I HAVE BEEN
in DANGER

IN THE SAME BOAT

I HAVE BEEN
in DANGER

CHERYL FOGGO

COTEAU BOOKS

WWW.COTEAUBOOKS.COM

Editor for the Series, Barbara Sapergia.
Edited by Barbara Sapergia.
Cover painting and interior illustrations by Aries Cheung.
Cover and book design by Duncan Campbell.
"In The Same Boat" logo designed by Tania Wolk, Magpie Design.
Printed and bound in Canada by Houghton-Boston, Saskatoon.

National Library of Canada Cataloguing in Publication Data

Foggo, Cheryl.
I have been in danger

ISBN 1-55050-185-2

1. Title.
PS8561.O3315 2001   JC813'.54   C2001-911224-6
PZ7.F6331H 2001

10 9 8 7 6 5 4 3 2

COTEAU BOOKS
401-2206 Dewdney Ave
Regina, Saskatchewan
Canada   S4R 1H3

available in the Canada and the US from:
Fitzhenry & Whiteside
195 Allstate Parkway
Markham, Ontario
Canada   L3R 4T8

The publisher gratefully acknowledges the financial assistance of the Saskatchewan Arts Board, the Canada Council for the Arts, including the Millennium Arts Fund, the Government of Canada through the Book Publishing Industry Development Program (BPIDP), and the City of Regina Arts Commission, for its publishing program.

For my three greatest blessings –
Clem, Chandra, and Miranda

CHAPTER 1

J ACKIE FELT A TICKLE ON HER FACE AND OPENED HER EYES. *A wasp was crawling along her cheekbone, moving toward her temple. It stopped very near her eye.*

"Don't sting me," she thought.

She lay perfectly still, face down, her left cheek pressed against the rough surface of the mountain. The wasp resumed its stroll, across her forehead and up into her hair. It hesitated for a moment, gave a loud buzz, then flew away.

Jackie was greatly relieved. Every part of her body hurt already.

"Good thing Sidney isn't here," she thought. Jackie's two-years-younger sister, Sidney, who was in Grade Four, was afraid of wasps. She always did the wrong thing, despite what they'd been taught in Junior Forest Wardens, when a wasp appeared near her. She screamed and leapt about and waved

her arms like an enormous, insane bird trying to achieve liftoff.

Immediately after having the thought about it being a good thing Sidney wasn't there, Jackie realized what a stupid thought it was. If Sidney had been there, Jackie would not be in this predicament.

She was lying on a bed of stones and twigs. The skin on her thighs and arms was stinging. Her head throbbed. The tickle on her face had not gone away when the wasp flew off. A small stream of blood from a cut above her eyebrow trickled down her cheek. Most of all, her right ankle felt like someone strong had tried to rip her foot from her leg.

An irritating sound, a continuous raspy moan, rose from deep inside her and escaped through her lips.

"How did I get here?" she wondered.

She closed her eyes again and bit on her bottom lip, trying to make the pain in her foot go away, trying to keep herself from throwing up.

Of course she was asking herself, how did I get here? But she wasn't wondering about how she got there, on the side of a mountain, lying on the twigs and stones.

She was thinking about her life and things that had happened.

WHEN JACKIE AND SIDNEY BAILEY were little girls, their favourite game didn't have a name. One of them would say something like, "Let's pretend we don't have any parents or anybody to take care of us." And the other one would say, "Yeah. And say nobody knew what had happened to them, so we had to live all by ourselves, and the city was too dangerous, so we ran away to the country."

On it would go from there. They knew how to survive (because of Junior Forest Wardens) sleeping outside or in abandoned shelters night after night. They would always be on the run, always hiding from the orphanage people.

"I can't go any farther tonight, Sister," one would say to the other. "My legs won't go another step."

"Me too, Sister," the other one would say. "Maybe we should sleep in this old barn. They'll never catch us here."

Sometimes they got food and clothes by asking people if they could help them out around their farms. Sometimes a kindly old couple who had always wanted children of their own would take them in and they would live there for a few days. But then the people who wanted to put them in the orphanage would find out where they were and they would have to run away again. They would leave a note for the kindly old couple and sneak away in the middle of the night.

"Come on, Sister," they would whisper, and taking each other by the hand, they would tiptoe away from the bedroom they had shared in the home of the old people.

Sometimes they played the game outside, wrapping themselves in old sleeping bags and flitting from tree to tree in their backyard, which had so many trees that it seemed like a real forest to them. And sometimes the game seemed so true, that Sidney would cry as they lay on the deck of the home they lived in with their mother and father, Mary and Earl. They would lie on the deck, looking up at the stars, eating crackers and thinking of how the kindly old couple would feel when they woke up in the morning to find the two little girls had gone. When Sidney started crying real tears, that's when Jackie would say they should stop playing. She never liked to see her little sister cry.

Then they would go inside and Earl would give them rice pudding with ice cream, or cookies with hot chocolate.

ONCE, JUST AS THEY WERE SCRAPING the last few grains of rice from the bowls, their mother came home from a council meeting at their school and saw the sleeping bags on the deck. By then it had started raining, and she was frowning when she dragged in the sopping, smelly bags.

"Why are the kids still up?" she asked Earl.

"They were having so much fun, I didn't want to interrupt them."

"Oh yeah, some fun!" Rice pudding flew from Sidney's

mouth. "Jackie said the old lady might die from a heart attack, from the sorrow of us being gone, and I started crying!"

Sidney saying this made Jackie nervous. Sometimes their mother would laugh about their silly games, and other times the smallest things seemed to upset her. That particular night she didn't think their crying about the imaginary old lady's potential heart attack was funny.

"I want you both in bed, teeth brushed, within three minutes."

Their parrot, Brid, screamed from the family room, repeating their mother's words. "Bed, Brushed, Three Minutes!"

The girls hurried off to the bathroom, after Jackie shot Sidney a look that asked, "Why don't you think before you speak?"

"It's a school night, for heaven's sake, Earl," they heard their mother say to their father.

"Well, it's only...." His voice trailed off. Jackie surmised that he had looked at the clock on the wall and seen that it was 9:50.

Standing side by side, Jackie and Sidney brushed their teeth. Sidney rinsed and spit in the sink, then perched on the edge of the bathtub, as she always did, waiting for Jackie to finish, because Sidney was always finished brushing teeth first.

She took her finger and began writing invisible words on the wall. This was a ritual she performed every night as she waited for Jackie to rinse and spit. She was leaving a note for her imaginary friend, Gala. She talked to Jackie at the same time.

"Jackie, what if the letter *l* and the letter *p* were switched around, so like, say North Pole would be North Lope?"

"I don't know." Jackie carefully rinsed her toothbrush and hung it up, then rinsed Sidney's as well, because she hadn't done it carefully. She was amazed at how quickly Sidney could forget something distressing, like their mother's mood, and think about something else. She watched Sidney as she traced letters.

"What are you telling Gala this time?"

"I'm reminding him to lock the window after he comes, so Ziggy can't get in." Ziggy was another of Sidney's imagined acquaintances. Gala was nice, but Sidney was afraid of Ziggy.

Jackie heard their mother's footsteps coming down the hall. She grabbed her sister's writing finger to stop her.

Their mother didn't like Sidney writing invisible notes to imaginary friends. "Go to bed now, 'kay, Sis?"

Sidney shrugged and went to bed and Jackie went down the hall to her bedroom too. She lay on the floor, then closed the door and pressed her ear against it, so she could hear what her parents were saying.

"Why do you let them work themselves up like that?"

"Mary, will you relax? They're just kids playing a game."

Her parents rarely argued. When they did, it was usually because Mary was worried about Jackie and Sidney, and Earl thought she was overreacting.

"People will think they're weird."

"Who do you think has binoculars aimed at our deck to see what our kids are doing? And even if someone did see them, who cares?"

Mary didn't seem to have an answer for this.

Jackie was tired that night and fell asleep on the floor.

CHAPTER 2

S IDNEY STOOD NEXT TO A LODGEPOLE PINE ON A PRECIPICE overlooking a richly green valley. It wasn't a tree like all the others that surrounded it. It was a much darker green, and much larger than its neighbours. It was the sheltering tree, the one its little sisters reached out for, leaned toward, counted on. It was Brid's tree. She and Jackie had selected it as Brid's tree after he died because it was so large and strong, a forever kind of tree. They had wanted to bury Brid there, but their mother had said she didn't think it was proper to dispose of pets' bodies on government property.

In the end, they'd had to settle for placing three of Brid's tail feathers in a deep hollow at the tree's roots and covering them with a large rock that they managed to squeeze into the hollow. They had surrounded the one large rock with many smaller ones, built a little mound, and placed a tiny cross, made from *twigs held together with twine, into the rocks. Then they had scouted around until they found another rock, just the perfect size, and pushed it into the hollow, blocking the entranceway to Brid's memorial. Only they knew where it was. Courtney Strachan-Smith didn't know, and she was Brid's first owner. Jackie and Sidney's parents didn't know. Even Chris didn't know.*

SIDNEY SHIELDED HER EYES FROM THE SUN, *which had been directly overhead when she'd left Camp Snowberry, but was now at the beginning of the goodbye side of day. A tiny rumble in her stomach reminded her that she'd had nothing to eat since breakfast. The quicker she found Jackie, the quicker they'd be back at camp, in plenty of time for supper. Her eyes darted across the landscape below. She took a few steps off the path to get a better look, seeing that the rocky slope was gradual for a short distance, then became steep, then fell away into nothingness. There was a cliff down there – a windswept, lonely cliff. One more step forward and her foot slipped. She scrambled backward, heart thumping. A fall down a slope like that would be deadly.*

Across the valley, trees and trees and trees. To her left, the path she had just climbed zigzagged down and out of sight, into a forest that stretched beyond far, and to her right, the path continued. In that direction, she could see a stream wandering through the trees. Behind her, impenetrable forest. She turned around, still scanning, searching for a glimpse of something blue. But there was nothing. In front, below, behind, above, there was no sign of her sister Jackie, or the blue shirt she was wearing when Sidney last saw her.

Sidney's own long-sleeved shirt, the red uniform of the Junior Forest Wardens˙ club she belonged to, clung to her, drenched with sweat. Her breath came in quick, gulping gasps. Her pack was heavy. Her small shoulders ached from carrying it and her legs ached from the rapid climb. The pack slipped from her left shoulder and she let it fall to the ground. She opened it, took out her whistle and gave a sharp blast. The shrill echo bounced all around her. She listened hard for the sound of Jackie's voice calling back, but the only reply was a crow screaming down at her from atop Brid's tree.

She blew the whistle again, louder and longer. Nothing.

Her sister was lost, and although Sidney wasn't lost, she was a long way from help and unsure of what to do. She could sit down, to catch her breath, to try to quell her fear, to get hold of her mind, which was racing. She could go back to the campsite. She knew where it was, and although it would be much faster going back than it had been coming, because it was mostly downhill, it would still take an hour and a half to retrace her steps. By then the afternoon would be old, and even though the teachers would be alarmed and would help search, she wouldn't know where to tell them to start looking. Because when Sidney had set out to look for Jackie, she had been absolutely sure she would find her at Brid's tree. But she hadn't found her there, and now Sidney didn't know what to do. Going back to the campsite would be the safe thing. For Sidney. But not for Jackie. They would search until it grew too dark and dangerous, and if they didn't find her, they would call off the search until daylight returned.

She thought about her sister, alone on the mountain, lying or sitting in the dark somewhere against a tree, and her heart went cold. She wasn't going back, not without Jackie. She turned and continued along the path. She didn't know where she was going, but she was going.

SIDNEY'S WORLD WAS FILLED WITH MAGIC, and there was no place more magical than a wood. She saw things among the trees that made her believe magical worlds were everywhere. Not just that magic existed, but that there was so much magic that you could walk down a thousand different mountain paths and find your way into a thousand different worlds. She saw things other people didn't see.

Once, when the children were hiking up toward Ptarmigan Cirque with Earl, Sidney allowed herself to fall behind. It was a hot day, but they were so deep in the forest that the sun was only a shimmer high above the canopy of the trees. She looked up and saw it as a filmy yellow blanket over the beautiful green net of the treetops. Little stray fragments of light slipped between the spaces in the net but were swallowed up before they could fall into her upstretched hands. The earth smelled damp and cool, and the sweet, sharp scent of wolf willow filled her nostrils and the breath inside her mouth and the air all around her skin and her hair.

She knew if she listened carefully she would hear something from a magical world calling to her. She closed her eyes and ears and heart to the sounds of this world and opened them to magic, and heard the tiniest musical sound, like a bell ringing. She opened her eyes and saw at her feet a cluster of small white flowers. Fairy bells. A shiver ran through her.

When you're in a magical place, time doesn't always work, and Sidney suddenly wondered how many minutes might have passed. She knew how stupid it was to get separated from your group when you were hiking, so she hurried along after her father and sister.

And there was Jackie, right around the next bend. She had stopped too. She was facing the downslope of the mountain, but not looking, because her eyes were closed and she was feeling the air with her hands. She looked up when she heard Sidney, and Sidney thought she looked so, so happy. Jackie smiled and took her sister's hand and they walked silently together. And not very much farther up the path, Earl was sitting on a stump waiting for them.

CHAPTER 3

JACKIE THOUGHT SHE SHOULD TRY TO MOVE AGAIN. *She had tried before, but something had happened, something in the way her ankle had refused to follow when she commanded the rest of her leg to move. The last thing she remembered was hearing a cry leave her throat and having the world go dark. Now here she was opening her eyes again, she didn't know how much later. The air was different. The sun had misplaced itself.*

She began to wonder how long she had been there. Had it been five minutes? An hour? A day? If someone had been looking for her, they should have found her by now. As soon as she had that thought, she pushed it aside. Of course people were looking for her.

Who, she wondered? Not Courtney or Erica, although they were the last people she remembered seeing. Not Carter.

Chris? She remembered something about Chris.

Sidney would send someone.

Mrs. Talmadge or Mr. Kingsley or Mrs. Waldren or the park wardens would come.

But no one had come yet, and she thought it had been a long time, and she thought she should try to move again, because she knew she wasn't safe.

That was one of the things she remembered from the first aid lessons at Junior Forest Wardens. She tried to run over the checklist in her head.

> *1. Find injured person.*
> *She was the injured person, and so far no one had found her, so that took care of that.*
> *2. Are we safe?*
> *She was quite certain that was the second thing on the checklist.*
> *— Check to see how the accident was caused.*
> *— Are we in danger?*
> *— Can I remove us from danger, or the danger from us?*

What was it about danger, and Chris, that she had remembered? His nose bleeding and his hand wrapped in tissue as he tried to stop it.

JACKIE AND SIDNEY had known Chris for so long that Sidney couldn't even remember the time before he became part of their lives. When Chris and Jackie were five, their fathers started their local Forest Wardens club together. Jackie and Chris earned the first badges ever awarded by the club.

After they earned their Bronze Badges, Jackie and Chris decided they wanted to cover their sleeves with every badge possible. They studied the manual together. They sat bent over poster paper, with their tongues sticking out from the corners of their mouths, and carefully coloured their Life Cycle of Four Insects posters. They practised knots and lashings on every piece of rope or cord they could find, and once got into trouble by tying the belt for Chris's mother's robe into six knots that no one could undo.

The badges began to pile up and Chris and Jackie started wearing their Junior Forest Warden uniforms every day, everywhere they went. To school, to church, to birthday parties. Jackie insisted on wearing hers underneath her tutu for ballet class. A long-sleeved red shirt doesn't go well under a tutu, and the effect of the shirt collar and rope bunched up on her shoulder gave Jackie a rather Hunchback of Notre Dame-ish look, but she didn't mind.

Chris refused to take his uniform shirt off at all, except for baths, and even then he would make his mother hang it on the doorknob so that it wouldn't leave his sight. Afraid the badges would fall off in the washing machine, he wouldn't allow his parents, Bob and Lindy, to wash it. He wore it to bed.

After a week it was stained with spaghetti sauce, apple juice, and peanut butter, which had dried into a most unattractive, crusty brown spot. By Friday the shirt had started to smell.

Unable to stand it any longer, Lindy stole into Chris's room that night, undid the buttons, slipped off the shirt, and whisked it away to the washer.

At three o'clock in the morning, the doorbell rang and Bob and Lindy bolted from their bed. They could see through the blinds that lights were flashing outside the window, as they both ran down the hallway, hearts pounding.

There was Chris, wearing only his underwear, opening the door to a tall police officer.

"What's going on?" Bob and Lindy gasped at the same time.

"We got a call from this address, concerning a robbery."

Lindy grabbed hold of Chris. "Are you okay?"

"No!" he cried, "Someone stole my uniform!"

CHAPTER 4

SIDNEY CONTINUED DOWN THE PATH, MOVING AS *quickly as care would allow. She didn't want to miss any signs that Jackie was nearby, or had gone that way. She also didn't want to move too quickly and risk tripping. What good would she be to Jackie if she fell and got hurt?*

The handful of trail mix she crunched on was better than nothing, but didn't do much to stop her from thinking about her mother's hamburgers. There would be no hope of getting back for supper now, she knew. She and Jackie would have to be content with leftovers.

Every once in a while she stopped to blow her whistle and listen to the sounds around her. But there were just the usual forest noises — birds chattering, wind through the trees, the hurried rustle of tiny forest creatures scurrying beneath their leaf blankets. No sounds or signs of Jackie.

Then, just after one particularly long blast of her whistle,

Sidney did hear a sound. Although far off in the distance, it filled her with dread.

Thunder.

IT WAS RAINING the day Sidney first noticed the change that had happened between Jackie and Chris.

She was lying on her stomach in the family room with paints, felt pens, and pencil crayons all spread out around her, making a picture of the world Gala lived in, which he had described to her in great detail. His world lacked electricity and was lit up entirely by fireflies and brilliant silver stars that streamed across the sky. Capturing the nighttime colours was difficult. The treetop house Gala shared with his mother and father and his twenty-seven brothers and sisters was blue, she knew that. But it was a very particular shade of blue, and the way the fireflies rose and fell as they flew around, illuminating Gala's house, caused the blue roof to change colour. It shimmered here and there a brilliant royal blue and then slipped back to midnight as the fireflies moved on. Not easy to capture on paper, and she was only half-listening to her parents talking as they moved around the house. Half-listening was more than she used to do, but since Lindy died the year before, many things in her world had changed. Paying more attention to what her parents were saying was just one of them.

"Do you think Chris is doing okay?" her mother was asking her father.

"Sure," he replied.

"Why?"

Her father seemed surprised by this question.

"What do you mean?"

"Why do you think he's doing okay?"

"Well. I just do. Bob would say something if he wasn't."

"Would Bob know if he wasn't? I'm not even sure Bob's doing okay."

"They're both doing as well as can be expected, Mary."

But Mary didn't seem satisfied with this.

"Jackie!" she shouted, and Jackie answered from some distant part of the house.

"Yeah?"

"Call Chris and ask him to come over, please."

That was the moment Sidney realized something else had changed.

Jackie came into the room and called Chris, as her mother requested. And although the look on her face said she didn't want to do it, she did it anyway, without protest. That's what upset Sidney. In the past, if Jackie hadn't felt like hanging out with Chris, she would have said so.

Sidney left her drawing and followed Jackie down the hall to her bedroom.

Jackie picked up a book.

"Hey," Sidney said.

"Hey," Jackie said back, but she didn't look up.

Sidney stood looking at her sister for a long time, but when Jackie continued to ignore her, she went down to the front door to wait for Chris.

When he arrived, the three of them went to the basement to play video games. Sidney sat between her sister and Chris and pondered how and when this change had snuck into her life, without her permission, as so many changes were doing. When had Chris and Jackie started saying "excuse me" to each other? When had Jackie started being extra nice to Chris, in that awkward way people save for those whom their parents want them to be nice to?

After a half-hour of searching for the Platinum Zolgarina Mask in the Old Silverwood Forest, Jackie grew tired of the game and left Chris and Sidney to play on their own.

Ordinarily, Sidney would have relished the opportunity to have Chris to herself, especially because she had been searching for the Platinum Mask for three weeks. Chris was the smartest person in their school, and if he couldn't find The Mask, no one could. But Chris's heart wasn't in the game either. She stole glances at him out of the corner of her eye. Something about the way his hair stuck up and cast a shadow on the wall whenever the lightning flashed, something about the silence all around them except for the sound of rain lashing the windows, made her suddenly very sad.

"Chris," she asked impulsively. "Do you believe in magic?"

Chris was the only person who didn't laugh at her on the camping trip two summers ago when Ziggy lost Sidney's shoes in the creek.

The thing she loved most about him was the way he always considered her questions carefully, as though they were important questions.

"What kind?"

"Like...like that there are other worlds and stuff. Or magical things from other places that can come to us. Or places where...stuff we've lost is waiting for us."

"I don't know. Do you?"

Sidney had talked with Chris about magic before, but this was different. There was something on her mind, something she'd been wanting to say to him, and this seemed like the moment.

"Maybe there are places where people who we think are dead are waiting for us to come find them."

Chris was quiet. Then he said, "You mean my mother?"

She nodded.

"She's not hiding, Sidney."

Sidney heard a noise in the laundry room. Her mother was transferring clothes from the washer to the dryer.

Chris went back to the video game, and a few minutes later Bob came to take him home.

FROM HER BEDROOM, Jackie heard Chris leaving.

"Goodbye, dear," her mother said to him. "I love you very much."

Jackie didn't hear Chris's response.

LATER, AS SIDNEY WAS GETTING READY FOR BED, her parents came into her room. They closed the door and sat on her bed, watching her put her colouring implements away. They both looked unhappy.

"You're nine years old now, Sidney. You have to start thinking about other people's feelings. You can't involve Chris in your fantasy games when it concerns the death of his mother." Earl was doing the talking. Mary had trouble speaking about Lindy.

"It's not a game," Sidney told them.

"It *is* a game. You know it's a game."

Sidney looked from one to the other. How could she make them understand?

"I'm not saying we could find her for sure if she was in another...world, but I'm just saying...."

Her mother finally found her voice.

"Listen." She took Sidney firmly by the arms and waited until she was looking into her eyes. "You're old enough now to understand the difference between fantasy and reality, and if I hear you teasing Chris like that again, I'll be very upset with you."

"I wasn't teasing Chris! I wouldn't do that."

"Sidney."

"Just because adults only know about certain kinds of magic doesn't mean there aren't other kinds."

Her parents looked at each other.

"What kinds of magic do we know about?" her father asked.

"When I asked you how the Tooth Fairy knows when I've lost a tooth, you said, 'By Magic.'"

SIDNEY HAD CRIED FOR HOURS after she went to bed that night. She couldn't stop thinking about all the lies they had told, which they were now saying were just "stories." As if that made it okay.

CHAPTER 5

.

THE DAY HOVERED BETWEEN LATE AFTERNOON AND
early evening and the thunderheads rolled closer.

*Sidney began to grow desperate, and more hasty, and less
careful. She skidded on some loose stones, lost her footing and
went down, breaking her fall with her hands.*

*When she was younger, she would have blamed the fall
on someone like Ziggy.*

*Tears rose. She fought them, but they fell anyway, right
alongside the first drops of rain.*

*"Idiot," she said aloud to herself. "You go sliding over a
cliff, who's going to help Jackie?"*

Her own words hit her like a slap.

"Sliding over a cliff."

*Suppose something had disturbed Brid's memorial and
Jackie had gone down that rocky slope, as they had done the*

summer before, looking for a good stone? Jackie wasn't wearing hiking boots. She didn't have any rope. Going down that cliff would have been a stupid thing to do, but what if Jackie had done it, and fallen and been hurt?

Sidney stood up and brushed away the pebbles that clung to her jeans. Panic and fear were the worst enemies of a person in a crisis. That was one of the first things she had learned. She made herself take a deep breath. Then she set her pack on the forest floor and rummaged through it until she found her raincoat and her flashlight. She didn't need it yet, but she would soon.

She slipped the coat on and clipped the flashlight to a ring on the pocket, then hoisted her pack once more, turned around and forced her burning legs back in the direction of Brid's tree.

BRID WAS NOT HIS NAME when he came to live with them, but both Jackie and Sidney thought Burpsie was a stupid name for any bird to have to live with, especially a bird as smart as he was. He could say more words than they could count, and both sisters believed without a doubt that he knew what each word meant. He proved that the day he renamed himself.

Back in those days, Courtney was still just a little girl, like all the other girls Jackie and Sidney knew. True enough, she usually stole something when she left the homes of her play-mates, but most people didn't notice. The things she stole were useless items, like old pairs of shorts or discarded dolls, things she probably would have been given if she'd asked for them. She had a beautiful smile and golden curls that were always tied up in bows, and she would visit the homes of her classmates and steal things from them and store them in a box under her bed. She never wore them or used them, but often at night, while her parents were screaming, she would slide the box out and look at them. One day she had come to school crying and Jackie had been the first to ask:

"What's wrong, Court?"

"My mom says I have to get rid of Burpsie."

Jackie knew who Burpsie was. She cringed at the name, as always, but said nothing to Courtney about that.

"Why?"

"She says she's tired of cleaning up after him."

Jackie had been to Courtney's home shortly after Courtney's father left and had seen Burpsie's cage. It was tiny and bent and always filthy. Burpsie was a very grumpy parrot. He would scream at her when she came near, things like, "You think I'm made of money?" or "Touch me again and I'll call the cops!"

But Jackie admired Burpsie's obvious intelligence, and despite the shrieking, she would stand near his cage and look in on him.

Courtney continued. "She says she can't stand the reek anymore. He doesn't stink, does he?"

Jackie shook her head no. Burpsie didn't stink. His cage certainly smelled like the worst morning breath mixed with the fumes from an outhouse, but that wasn't Burpsie's fault. He was always cleaning himself.

Courtney's tears fell faster now.

"My dad gave Burpsie to me for Christmasss," she wailed. "And now she says we have to put him to sleeeepppp. We tried to sell him, but no one wants him because he swearrrrsss!"

"We'll buy him," Jackie said.

Jackie and Sidney had a terrible time convincing Mary and Earl that they should take the swearing parrot in. Mary didn't want a pet any more than Courtney's mother did, certainly not one that cursed and shrieked, and especially not one named Burpsie. But the girls were relentless and made many promises, and their parents gave in, on one condition, Mary said.

"You have to change his name."

Jackie and Sidney agreed, because they too believed that part of the bird's grumpiness stemmed from hearing himself referred to as "Burpsie." They took money from their bank accounts and pooled it and bought many things for him, including a big cage with three perches. They also took name books out of the library and pored over them. They wanted an African name because he was an African Grey.

One day while he explored his new cage, Jackie was doing homework as Sidney thumbed through the name books. Jackie sighed heavily and Sidney looked at her sister.

"What's wrong?"

"This is so *dull.*" She was doing math sheets. Page after page of them as a punishment for not having done the ones she'd been assigned the week before.

"If I don't hand it in tomorrow, Mrs. McRae will bridrify me even worse."

"Bridrify" was a word Jackie or Sidney had made up. They could no longer remember which of them was the first to say it, but it was a perfect word to describe how you felt when the teacher told you off in front of the whole class, or when you came last in a race, or when your fingers were so cold you felt like they were going to fall off, but you knew it was your own fault because you'd lost your gloves again. There was no word in the English language that was as good in so many different situations, and they both used it frequently.

Jackie sighed again. "I'm totally bridrified."

Brid, who was still Burpsie then, had been drinking water from his lovely, clean water dish.

"Bridrified," he said.

Jackie and Sidney both laughed, threw down their books, and went over to his cage.

"Bridrified. I'm Bridrified," Brid said.

"Courtney's mother bridrified you, didn't she?" Jackie asked.

He repeated, "I'm bridrified." He also spat out a swear.

"Mom!" Sidney shouted toward the kitchen. "Our bird says he's bridrified!"

"That's a good name," Mary called back.

After that the former Burpsie became Bridrified, and eventually it was shortened to Brid.

People who didn't know Jackie and Sidney always assumed that "Brid" was just a misspelling of "Bird," but that didn't bother any of them, especially not Brid. It took time, but Brid changed. He only shrieked at people he didn't like. He still delighted in croaking, "I'll give you something to cry *about!*" to guests, but he always finished with a cackling laugh. And eventually he only swore when his seed dish was empty.

CHAPTER 6

W HEN SIDNEY GOT BACK TO THE TREE, SHE KNELT *down to look at the hollow. Their round, perfect rock was gone. She bent low and peered inside, and saw Brid's memorial safe and intact. She slipped her hand into the hollow, pushed aside their carefully stacked stones, and felt around until her fingers found one of Brid's feathers. Brid had always brought good luck to Sidney and Jackie, and if she ever needed luck, it was now. She scrambled to her feet again and brushed the dirt and pine needles from her knees, clutching that little piece of Brid in her hand.*

THE MEMORIAL HAD BEEN JACKIE'S IDEA. They would find a place where fairy bells grew, a magical place that would keep Brid's spirit, and they would hide the tail feathers there.

Sidney had stopped crying and her face had lit up.

"Yeah. And we could keep going back there. And maybe if the magic is working, we'll find our way into a world. And even if Brid isn't there, even if it's not the world where dead pets go, it'll be like Brid's spirit led us there."

Jackie nodded.

That's what they had done. On their next camping trip in the mountains, they found the tree and hid the feathers. When they finished blocking up the entrance to Brid's magical memorial resting spot, and singing the song Sidney had made up to commemorate the occasion, Jackie said, "Don't cry, Sister."

And Sidney laughed.

CHAPTER 7

*C*an *I remove us from the danger, or the danger from us?
Jackie wasn't us, she was just her, but she was sure the
answer to the question was no, we are not safe. She thought
she should try to remove herself from the danger.*

*With a great effort, she rolled over onto her back, to try
to get a better sense of how far down the mountain she had
fallen. Quite far, she saw. Also that she had been very lucky.
About seven metres below her the mountain slope ended and
became a cliff. Her tumble down the mountainside had been
stopped by a small, sturdy tree, no taller than a bush, but
strong enough that it had prevented her from sliding down
and over the cliff. All around her there were wide-open places
of nothing but bits of scrub grass desperate enough to spring
from the rocks. If she had slid down those places, nothing
could have helped her.*

She raised her head a little, then tried to sit up by placing her hands under her back and pushing. Her hands slid out from underneath her and she slipped, just a bit, but fear wrung her. She reached out and clutched at the little bush. When she was sure she had a firm grip, she forced herself to twist her head around to look up the mountain, to where she knew the path was. She couldn't see it, and her heart sank, because she knew she couldn't be seen, either.

She was unable to think clearly. The pain in her ankle rang so loudly in her brain that all other thoughts were drowned out. She tried to remember what she had learned in Junior Forest Wardens that might help her now, but whether on purpose or not, she had forgotten.

A drop of rain fell on her arm.

WHEN JACKIE AND CHRIS were eleven years old, and Sidney was nine, they were on the six o'clock news. They'd gone for a hike in Banff with their Forest Wardens club and Chris had spotted a small fire smouldering in the trees. They all helped put the fire out with their water bottles, then stamped out the embers and notified the park wardens. TV crews had come to interview them, and Chris was the hero, because they said it was his eagle eyes that had spotted the fire in the first place. All the Junior Forest Wardens received a Fire Honour Badge, and Chris was so excited he'd taken his to school the next day. His classmates crowded around and asked him how many TV cameras had been there, and they all wanted to hold his badge.

Then, at recess, Courtney called him "eagle eyes" in such a way that it signalled to everyone that his moment in the spotlight had ended. In an instant, people were calling him "eagle boy." "eagle nose," "eagle butt," and finally, "bird crap." Chris put his badge in his pocket.

After that, he always kept it with him. He never pulled it out to look at when he was at school, but sometimes, when he found life difficult, he would remind himself that it was there.

When Sidney hopped on the bus after school that afternoon, *her* classmates were still buzzing with the excitement of her forest adventure. Her best friend, Kate, was retelling the story, turning Sidney into a great forest fire warrior – Sidney had put out a raging inferno with the help of a helicopter and had been flown to LA to appear on three talk shows.

Jackie was sitting at the back of the bus with Courtney and her friends.

Chris sat alone.

THAT NIGHT, Sidney crept into her father's office, where

he sat with a stack of papers in his lap. Some of the papers had drifted to the floor, but he hadn't seemed to notice. Sidney picked them up, then took the others from him and placed them neatly on his desk. She crawled onto his lap.

"Daddy, are you sad?"

"A little," he said. "Are you?"

She nodded.

They were silent for a few moments before Sidney asked, "Why does Jackie want to quit Junior Forest Wardens?"

Her father answered, "I don't know."

ONE DAY COURTNEY CAME TO SCHOOL wearing makeup, a fake nose ring, and a shirt that said, "Screw You!" Mr. Kingsley made her go home to change.

The world shifted after that. Some of the boys started receiving phone calls from girls pretending to be other girls. But only some. Groups were formed. Courtney decided which people belonged where. She became, at the same time, both the most popular girl in the class and the least liked. She was ruthless. She was cruel. People who cared about being popular were terrified of her but dreamed of being her friend.

This all seemed very amusing to Jackie and Chris at first. Their Junior Forest Wardens club had sponsored a female wolf who lived in the Kananaskis, and they had studied wolf pack behaviour. The biggest, toughest, meanest, most cunning wolf in the pack was known as the alpha. Chris started referring to Courtney as the alpha. Erica was the beta – the second in command. Sidney laughed along with Jackie and Chris too, although she didn't really understand what they were talking about. Everyone in her class liked each other.

But soon enough, it didn't seem funny anymore. Jackie started to feel uneasy as she approached the bus stop each morning. Seeing the green paint on the doors to the school made her stomach hurt. She began to hate that particular shade of green. She found herself on the fringes of various groups. She couldn't find her place. Some days Courtney and Erica would invite her to sit with them in the library at lunchtime. Other days she would be halfway seated into a chair at their table and they would say, "Oh, Lindsay's sitting there." At first when this happened, she would join Chris, who had no group, at the table where he sat alone.

No one knew how Courtney made her decisions. Maybe Chris was too tall. Maybe he was too smart. Maybe his elbows were too pointy. Maybe he had a father who hadn't left him. Maybe it was Junior Forest Wardens. No one knew why. They only knew Chris was nobody, and only nobodies ate lunch with him. After it happened a few times, Jackie went to eat her lunch in the girls' washroom. She didn't want to be the girl eating her lunch in the girls' washroom. She didn't want to be the girl on the fringe. She didn't want to be the girl sitting with the boy no one wanted. She wanted to be normal. She didn't want to be weird. She wanted to be normal.

CHAPTER 8

JACKIE'S ARMS WERE GROWING TIRED.

"*If you are lost, hug a tree! Choose a tree and stay near it – Someone will find you.*"

She clung to her little bush/tree, because she had remembered learning it was a good thing to do.

"*Stay with your tree.*"

But she didn't know how much longer she could hold on. She was shaking.

She was wet.

"*Oh God, help me,*" *she said.*

She thought about Chris, his nose, the blood seeping through his fingers. What had happened? She tried to make herself remember. She knew it had something to do with her.

She cringed as a crack of thunder sounded over her head.

"*I'm sorry, Chris.*"

Jackie thought she heard a whistle, but it was far off and strange sounding, slightly off-key, like a dream or the sound a child makes when he's playing rocket ship blast-off. Or like Papa Williams imitating Brid imitating the sound of the kettle whistling.

JACKIE'S PAPA WILLIAMS was the best whistler she knew. He could do every bird call that existed, and when Grandpa Bailey hauled out his saxophone at family gatherings, Papa Williams would whistle along to every tune, in perfect pitch.

Nana and Papa Williams lived in the same house they'd lived in when Jackie and Sidney's mother was a little girl. It was a big, rambling house, and although they had kept it neatly painted and repaired, it had never been renovated. Both girls loved the old house for its age. The doorknobs were made of glass, the floors were made of ancient hardwood that creaked and smelled of polish, the bathtub had little feet with curled-over toes. The house had hidden cupboards large enough to hide in, and steep, narrow staircases that led to high-up rooms where you could pretend you didn't hear when the adults called and said it was time to go home. Jackie and Sidney had many sleepovers in the big bed with the soft down covers. They giggled long after all the lights had been turned off, and

Sidney told Jackie stories of the magical inhabitants of Nana and Papa's house.

Sidney and Jackie knew how lucky they were to have all four grandparents – Grandma and Grandpa Bailey, and Nana and Papa Williams. Some of their friends didn't know their grandparents, or, like Chris, had none living. It didn't seem fair to them that they had four grandparents and Chris had none, especially after his mother died.

Papa was a much smaller man than Grandpa Bailey – Jackie had surpassed him in height when she was eleven. He had a deep, rumbly voice, which always surprised people upon first meeting. He was small, so they expected a small voice, and when he spoke, cashiers at the grocery store would look twice to see if that rolling, thundery sound had really come from him. He was very dark, too. The colour of the bark on an old tree.

Jackie envied Papa's colour. No one looked at him, in the grocery store or at the park or anywhere, and wondered "what" he was. They could see by looking. She envied Sidney, whose skin was light brown and whose hair was more than wavy, it was curly. No one ever said to Sidney, in that surprised way, "Is that your mother?" No one said stupid, hurtful things about Black people around Sidney, unless they meant to because they were idiots. No one ever asked Sidney the insulting question, "What are you?" They knew, by looking at her from the outside. Not so with Jackie.

Papa always said that Jackie was like him, and it was probably true that she and he, more than anyone else in either family, kept their secrets, hid their feelings, shared with few. Sometimes, when all the aunts and uncles and cousins were together at Nana and Papa's house, which was often, Jackie and Papa would slip away from all the noise and go for a walk outside.

Nana and Papa's old house was on an old street, and in the summer the enormous trees that lined the sidewalks on both sides met and formed a canopy over the top. Jackie and Papa would walk beneath the canopy and talk a little, but not too much, and that's the way they both liked it. Some of the neighbours they greeted were old and had lived on the street for a long time, but most were not. Many were couples with children younger than Jackie and Sidney, who had bought the old houses and made the insides different, to look like new houses. Some were young couples with no children, who bulldozed the old houses and trees and put brand new, bigger houses in their places. Jackie was glad Nana and Papa's house was still old and she wanted it always to be that way.

"Can I live in your house when I'm older, Papa?" she had asked one day when they were on one of their walks.

"Well, I think that would be real nice. Real nice."

"I'll buy it from you, and you and Nana can live with me. I'll take care of you."

"What you wanna take care of two old people for? You'll have your own family and a husband and all that."

"No. I won't."

This is what Jackie always said when there was talk of her growing up and getting married.

She never bothered explaining why. She knew people thought it was because she was twelve and boys were yucky. They always chuckled patronizingly, and exchanged looks that said, "Oh ho, isn't that cute, Jackie thinks boys are yucky. Nudge, nudge, wink, wink, for now."

Jackie didn't think boys were yucky, she liked them. Sometimes when Carter Leavitt stood close to her, a wild, sort of nice, but sort of awful feeling would sweep over her, and she would try to think of ways to keep him there. And sometimes, when she caught him looking at her, she would look back at him, for the tiniest moment. And in that moment, she would wonder what it would be like to keep looking, to look at his eyes and his mouth and his face for a long time, but of course she wouldn't. She would look away, and so would he. And sometimes, when Chris wasn't around, she would even giggle at Carter or some other boy's stupid jokes, in the way she was learning to do from Courtney and Erica and their friends.

The reason she wouldn't grow up and marry somebody with eyes like Carter Leavitt's was Chris. When she and Chris were six years old, they had promised to get married some day. Now that Jackie was older, she knew she wouldn't marry Chris. She didn't get any kind of feeling when he stood close to her. But she couldn't hurt his feelings by marrying someone else, either, so that was that.

Papa didn't laugh when she said, "No, I won't." He was the only one who didn't. Jackie loved her Papa.

CHAPTER 9

THE DARK CLOUDS HAD SWALLOWED UP MOST OF *what remained of the daylight.*

Sidney had tied her rope to Brid's tree with a clove hitch and secured it to her waist with a double figure eight, and was making her way carefully down the slope. The pebbly surface was now wet and finding secure footing was next to impossible. Without her hiking boots and rope, she would have been in serious danger. Even so, she had to move cautiously, her body turned sideways to the slope, inch by inch, easing the rope through her right hand as she held the flashlight in her left and scanned the beam back and forth in all directions. A wind had come up by now, and although she was calling hoarsely — "Jackie! Jackie!" — her voice was smothered and carried away so that she could barely hear it herself. She halted her slow progress, fumbled for her whistle, and when she blew, the sound rang out much more clearly than her feeble cries. She waited, listening for a reply.

There was no response from Jackie, but Sidney heard something else, faintly in the distance. At first she wasn't sure, then she was – it was the rapid beat of a helicopter's propeller. Someone was searching for them!

Sidney aimed her beam in the direction the sound was coming from and began frantically waving it back and forth. She heard a rumble. The helicopter was coming closer! The rumble became a roar and her heart sank – it was thunder. She slipped off her pack and pulled off her coat. Frantically, she swung it around and around over her head, waving its yellow brightness back and forth.

"Here, here I am," she called, but the wind snatched her small, ineffectual words and snuffed them out. The sound of the helicopter receded. It had passed near, but not near enough. She knew it wouldn't be back, the storm made it dangerous for the pilot. She was on her own.

A jagged stream of brilliant white light seared her eyes. Seconds later, a great crack of thunder, like a gunshot, blistered her ears. Sidney dropped to her knees, cowering. In that moment of illumination, she had seen what she was – a tiny little person, a speck on a vast mountain in an endless universe.

As SIDNEY approached her tenth birthday, she came to

the conclusion that ten was an insignificant number, as ages went. She complained about it to Grandpa Bailey one day as they pulled weeds together in the little rock garden he and Grandma had built.

"I feel like I'm turning nothing," she said. "It's just an in-between age. I'm not a little kid, I'm not a teenager. I'm a *'tween!* How would you like it if you were called a 'tween?"

"Don't suppose I would," he replied.

She went on. "I'm a nothing. I'm a grain of dust."

"We all are," was his surprising response. He tipped back in his chair and pressed his fingertips together, looking off toward the begonias. "We're nothing and we're everything, all at once."

Sidney didn't know what he was talking about, and the look she gave him told him so.

He continued. "I'm just one of billions of people who've lived in this world, man. So are you. None of us are more than specks. But each of us is God's whole heart, too."

Sidney shrugged. "I guess." She drove her little trowel into the soft earth and scooped out the long, fat root of a milkweed. Grandpa usually had interesting things to say, but she wasn't sure how this particular thought connected to her situation. She glanced up at him and saw that he was watching her.

"I got something for you," he said. "Early birthday present."

He went into the house and returned with a small, rectangular box. Sidney opened it and out slipped Grandpa's Swiss Army Knife.

Her mouth flew open. "Grandpa!" she shrieked, and flung her arms around him.

CHAPTER 10

THE RUMBLE OF THE THUNDER FADED AWAY AND THE *sounds of the mountain settled in around Sidney once more. Rain on rocks, rain through trees, rain rushing by in gurgling little streams through the pebbles.*

She was small and the mountain was large. But she wasn't giving up. That's what Grandpa meant.

In the brief minutes without the protection of her raincoat, she had become soaked to the skin and begun to shiver with cold. She slipped the coat on, felt in the pocket to make sure Brid's feather was still there, gripped her rope, and got to her feet once more.

Sidney continued her slow descent.

GRANDPA BAILEY had been a professional musician when he

was young. He was the saxophone player in a band whose other musicians were Black, and with whom he travelled all around western Canada, playing Louis Armstrong and Duke Ellington songs.

"But," he said to Sidney on the day he gave her the knife, "we had to know a lot of different kinds of music, because in those small towns we played back then, sometimes the people didn't want to hear Louis Armstrong. They wanted to hear polkas or country music. We could play it all, man."

He loved to tell stories of his days playing with Bobby Parker and the Moonstones, and Sidney loved to hear them. He referred to jobs as gigs. He spun endless tales to Sidney about his gigs with the band. He could imitate the way Spider Mapp, the drummer, walked, and the way Loopie Mayes, the bass player, talked. Jackie sometimes grew tired of hearing about the gigs and would drift off to read a book, but Sidney would stay endlessly and laugh out loud at the story of how Vern Franklin, the lead guitarist, had once accidentally played an entire gig with his fly unzipped and his leopard print underwear peeking through. She laughed no matter how many times he told the story.

Eventually, Grandpa met Grandma and got married and didn't want to travel anymore, but there weren't enough music gigs in Calgary to keep the band together.

Loopie and Spider and Vern wanted to settle down too, and took jobs with the railroad.

"All of them at the railroad?" Sidney asked.

"Yep, all of them, man," Grandpa replied.

"Why?"

"That was about the best gig the brothers could get in those days. Unless they played in a band. Railroad was better than pluckin' chickens."

Grandpa always referred to Black men as his "brothers." This embarrassed Jackie. He would say to the kid who worked at Safeway, "Thank you, brother," and the kid would look at him funny.

Jackie once complained privately to Sidney about this.

"I wish Grandpa wouldn't call Black men brothers. They think he's crazy."

"No, they don't. And besides," Sidney said, "if Grandpa didn't feel like he was one of the brothers, then he wouldn't have taken a gig at the railroad, and then he wouldn't have met Papa there, and they wouldn't have become friends, and then Mom and Dad never would have met and we wouldn't exist."

Jackie pondered this and saw the logic in it.

"Still, does he have to do it with people he doesn't even know?"

Sidney shrugged.

ALL GRANDPA'S BANDMATES found jobs as porters on the railroad, and it was Loopie Mayes who got Grandpa an interview. Only Grandpa got a job not as a porter, but as a manager, with higher pay.

"Because he was White," Mary had answered when Sidney asked her why.

The next time Sidney saw Grandpa Bailey, she asked him if that was true and he said yes.

"Were your friends mad?"

"Who wouldn't be?" he asked. "Loopie thought about quitting, but there wasn't much else. Porter was the best a brother could do."

Grandpa didn't enjoy the stories of the railroad so much and neither did Sidney, so they usually went back to music and his saxophone. He showed her how he had used the Swiss Army Knife to tighten things up when the instrument needed it, or to pry the felt pads off when they needed changing. The knife had gone everywhere with him, and now it went everywhere with her.

She took it to school once, with disastrous results.

THE SCHOOL SIDNEY AND JACKIE ATTENDED was very old, built of sandstone, and for some reason, although it was a four-storey building, the student bathrooms were located in the basement.

One day, Kate and Sidney were asked to take the attendance cards to the office, and Kate suddenly had to go to the bathroom very badly. She stood there with her legs crossed, hopping up and down on one foot.

"Well come on, if you have to go that bad!" said Sidney, heading for the basement stairs. "What are you waiting for?"

Kate remained where she was, a look of panic on her face.

"I can't. If I take one more step, there will be an incident!"

"You can't just stand there and pee your pants!" Sidney hissed. "You're not in kindergarten!"

Kate tried to walk, still with her legs crossed. She looked like a confused duck.

Sidney grabbed her by the shirt and dragged her into the staff bathroom, which was right there.

"We're not s'pose ta be in here!" Kate protested

"It's either this or the incident. Now hurry!" Sidney urged.

And they would have been in and out of there with no problem, if Kate hadn't had the very annoying habit of wearing a ring on every single finger every single day, and of taking them all off and laying them along the sink before she entered a cubicle, for fear one of her rings might drop into the toilet. This ritual she performed very rapidly, still rocking back and forth on her crossed legs.

"Hurry up!" Sidney said.

While Kate was in the cubicle, Sidney picked up one of the rings and held it to her nose, to see how it would look as a nose ring. It slipped from Sidney's fingers and she cracked her knuckles on the paper towel dispenser trying to save it, but it went straight into a wide slot in the ancient heat register.

Kate was very angry.

"You know how important those rings are to me!" She pressed one eye to the slot, but could see nothing but darkness.

They couldn't ask the caretaker for help – they weren't supposed to be in that bathroom in the first place.

Kate began to weep. "It was my Ring of Time."

She refused to calm down until Sidney promised to bring her Swiss Army Knife to school the next day, to use the screwdriver attachment to remove the heat register from the wall.

Sidney managed to keep her knife well hidden in her pocket the next day, although she found her hand strayed to it many times, and she would close her fingers around it, enjoying the thrill of knowing it was there.

When school was out, she posted Kate as a guard and ducked into the bathroom. They had a plan in case anyone tried to go in. Kate would warn Sidney, stalling for enough time to allow her to slip into a cubicle and pull her feet up out of sight.

But several things went wrong. First of all, Kate was nervous. Her asthma had been flaring up that day and Sidney could hear her wheezing. Secondly, it had been a long time since the screws had been undone, and it took forever for Sidney to loosen them. She had just barely managed to remove the cover of the heat register when she heard Kate say, in a strained, high-pitched voice, "Oh hello, Mrs. Talmadge. Uhhm. Uhhm. Uhhm."

She was trying to buy time for Sidney, but clearly her brain had turned into mashed potatoes.

"What is it, Kate?" asked Mrs. Talmadge's voice.

"Uhhm."

"Can't she think of something other than uhhm?" Sidney muttered to herself. She propped the heat register cover as best she could, then dashed into the cubicle and closed the door.

"Uhhm. I think the bathroom's being painted right now," she heard Kate say.

"No, it's not. You'd better hurry, or you'll miss the bus."

The door opened, Mrs. Talmadge came in, and her heavy footsteps caused the loose cover to come crashing down on her foot. There was quite a lot of noise, what with the clatter of the metal cover, Mrs. Talmadge's howl of pain, and Kate shouting "uhhm, uhhm, uhhm" in a shrill, hysterical tone.

The secretary, the caretaker, and several teachers came running.

Sidney and Kate were in serious trouble. Everyone was especially annoyed when they discovered the ring had come from a plastic $1.25 machine outside the mall entrance. The worst thing for Sidney was having her knife confiscated. The school, of course, had rules about people bringing weapons on the premises, and despite Sidney's pleas, they locked it away in a safe.

"You'll get it back at the end of the year," Principal Kingsley said firmly.

Sidney's parents refused to intervene on her behalf. They believed in letting their children learn by suffering the natural consequences of their actions. Sidney thought to herself that her mother believed she was too young to own a knife anyway and was secretly glad the knife was gone.

CHAPTER 11

THE HOOD ON SIDNEY'S RAINCOAT IMPEDED HER vision. *Frustrated, she threw it off, but then the rain slashed at her face, making it even more difficult to see.*

Sidney's Swiss Army Knife was clipped to her jacket. She carefully pulled out the tweezers hidden in a tiny compartment of the knife and used them to clamp the brim of the hood back, out of the way. That was better. She carried on down the slope.

The beam from her flashlight was strong, but its light cast only so far. Sidney was deeply worried. If she was wrong and Jackie hadn't come this way, she had no hope of finding her before nightfall. The dreadful knowledge that she would be spending the night alone on the mountainside had begun to settle over her.

Another brilliant flash broke, followed seconds later by a crack of thunder.

From the corner of her eye, Sidney caught sight of something blue off to the right. Was it a plastic bag? She held up her flashlight and shone it in that direction. There was nothing resembling a foothold, nothing but slippery shale interrupted by a lone little bush, which the blue item seemed to be caught in. Sidney lowered herself to her hands and knees. Checking to see that her knot was secure, and now clamping the flashlight between her teeth, she began to crawl toward the bush.

What was it? Not a plastic bag, she saw that now. It was a shoe. It was Jackie's shoe!

IN THE END, Grandpa Bailey and Papa Williams came to Sidney's rescue. Grandpa reminded Earl that when he was a little boy he had broken a school window with his BB gun.

"That was an accident, Dad," Earl said.

"Well, so was this, man."

Mary put her hand on her hip and peered at Grandpa. "I swear, if those kids painted your toenails red while you slept and told you it was an accident, you'd believe them."

"Course I would," said Grandpa. "Now, come on, Mary, you know she didn't mean any harm. It wasn't an accident, maybe, but it was a mistake. Kids make mistakes."

Papa looked up from the magazine he was reading.

"You keep saying you want her to grow up, Mary," he rumbled. "That knife makes her feel grown up."

Mary looked at Earl. "They're ganging up on us. Didn't I tell you if we got married we'd spend the rest of our lives being bullied by them?"

Earl laughed. Sidney, who was listening to all this from behind the door, smiled to herself.

Grandpa wrote a note to Mr. Kingsley, explaining that it was he who had given the knife to Sidney and that the incident was partly his fault because he had failed to impress upon his granddaughter the importance of using the knife only in the most appropriate circumstances. Then he wrote up a contract, which Sidney signed, promising that she would never bring the knife to school again. Mr. Kingsley relented.

Sidney had her knife back. She continued to carry it everywhere, except for school.

Good old Papa. Good old Grandpa.

CHAPTER 12

S IDNEY CRAWLED FORWARD AS QUICKLY AS SHE COULD, *and there, still clinging to her tree, she found her sister. She knelt over Jackie's still form.*

"Jackie. Jackie!" she called, but Jackie didn't respond.

1. *Find injured person.*
   Done.
2. *Are we safe?*
   Probably not. Can't do anything about that right now.
3. *Is the person breathing?*
   Sidney leaned closer to Jackie's face. Her skin was an unnatural colour, there was a cut over her left eye, but yes, she was breathing.
4. *Is there serious bleeding?*

Sidney quickly scanned Jackie's body. She had scrapes and abrasions everywhere, but none were oozing.

5. Is the person unconscious?

"Jackie, I'm here. I'm here. Please wake up."

Jackie's eyelids fluttered. Sidney touched her sister's skin. It was cold, even colder than Sidney expected. She had dry clothes in her pack, but it would do no good to try to dress Jackie here. The clothing would be soaked in moments. Also, Sidney knew she shouldn't try to move Jackie until she could figure out if her spine was injured. But she had to try to warm her somehow. The rain was still driving down on her, numbing her fingers. She slipped her pack off her back, and with shaking hands opened it up. She found the thin, waterproof, thermal blanket, still folded into the compact plastic case she had placed it in when the Junior Forest Wardens had studied the emergency supplies unit the summer before.

She unfolded the blanket and covered her sister's chilled form, then slipped off her raincoat once more and placed it over the blanket.

"Can you hear me, Jackie? It's Sidney. I'm here. I've found you. You're gonna be okay now."

Sidney looked at Jackie's foot, which seemed to be sticking out at an odd angle. The blue shoe she had first spotted was stretched tight. The foot inside it was swollen and the shoe bulged.

Sidney tried to untie the laces, but the rain had soaked the knots and they wouldn't budge. She unclipped her knife again and flicked open the sharpest blade, then very carefully, trying not to move Jackie's foot, began slicing through the knots. Despite her care, the ankle jiggled slightly.

Jackie cried out.

"It's me, Jackie," Sidney said.

A cracked, croaky sound came from Jackie's lips.

"Where's Chris?"

THE COMMUNITY ASSOCIATION in Sidney, Jackie, and Chris's neighbourhood held a dance for twelve-to-fifteen-year-olds every three months. They called these dances "Gum Drops." Jackie once heard Mrs. Talmadge tell Mary the organizers were trying to give the neighbourhood children something to do that would keep the drugs and booze and troublemakers from other neighbourhoods away, and stop Courtney and her friends from hanging around the strip mall smoking. She hadn't mentioned Courtney and Erica and Lindsay by name, but Jackie knew that was who she meant.

Many times, Sidney heard Jackie and Chris laughing at the twelve-year-olds who went to the dances to play at being older. It was pathetic, they agreed. They were above it.

So Sidney was shocked the day Jackie asked their parents if she could attend the next Gum Drop dance.

Earl had said no immediately.

"Dad, why not?"

"I've driven by those dances. They've got all kinds of older boys driving around there, probably sixteen, seventeen years old. Probably drinking and everything."

"Dad! They have to show ID. There are no sixteen- and seventeen-year-old boys there."

"I've seen them."

"They're just dropping off their younger siblings. Think about it! What seventeen-year-old wants to go to a dance with twelve-year-olds? Fifteen-year-olds don't even want to go, and they're allowed."

This was a clever thing for Jackie to point out. Earl had to admit it was probably true that no self-respecting seventeen-year-old, who had his dad's car for the night, would want to hang out with twelve-year-old kids from the elementary school.

He still looked highly doubtful, but Jackie noticed her mother hadn't said anything.

Jackie turned to her. "Everyone goes."

This too was clever. "Everyone" meant "all the normal kids."

Mary asked, "Who else will be there?"

Jackie had to be careful. She knew what her mother

was thinking. Is that horrible Courtney Strachan-Smith going to be there? And, of course, Courtney Strachan-Smith would be there. And it was Courtney Strachan-Smith who had said, casually, to Jackie at school the day before, "You goin' to the Gummy?"

Jackie knew the question was really an offer. Come be one of us. And Jackie was very, very tired of eating her lunch in the washroom. And she was tired of feeling like she didn't belong. And she thought about what it would be like to be one of those girls, and she thought maybe it would be better than being who she was. So she had said back, just as casually, "Yeah."

But now she had to be careful how she answered her mother's questions.

"Kids from school. Elizabeth Kinnie and Dallas Ogilvie."

This was good, and she saw a flicker of approval on her mother's face. Elizabeth's mother and Dallas's mother worked on the school council with Mary. Jackie went on, knowing her mother was still wondering.

"Erica and them will probably be there."

She knew that her mother knew that "and them" meant Courtney.

The flicker of approval disappeared. Mary didn't know Erica's mother, and Courtney's mother never did things like volunteer on the school council.

"Is Chris going?" her mother asked.

Jackie's first instinct was to say something sarcastic, like, "Of course, Mother, you know old crazy legs Chris, always the first at the dance and the last to go home. Old social butterfly Chris." But because she was being careful, she caught herself in time. What was her mother thinking? she wondered.

"I don't think so," Jackie replied.

"I don't like the looks of those dances," her father said.

"If Chris is going, she can go," Mary said.

Jackie tried to figure out what her mother was up to. Was she trying to help Chris by getting him to the dance, where he would be miraculously transformed into Mr. Happy Happy? Or did she think there was no way in the world he would go, and it was her way of preventing Jackie from going? Jackie wasn't sure. But if it were the latter, she would prove her mother wrong.

Chris was puzzled by Jackie's request – at first – then he thought she was joking, so he laughed. Then he said no.

"You wouldn't have to dance," Jackie pleaded. "They need people to take tickets at the door."

Chris was about to say no again when a thought popped into his mind. Was Jackie asking him to go to the dance with her? He didn't think she was. That didn't seem possible. But maybe she was. She had been very distant. Maybe she missed him, the way he missed her.

"Well...." he said.

"Please, Chris?"

He agreed to take tickets at the door.

And so Chris found himself in attendance at a dance for the first time since he was in Grade One and had gone to a school family dance with his mother and father.

Much to his surprise, he did not hate being there. The first half-hour he was very busy, and although most of the people he knew who came in and handed him their tickets seemed surprised to see him, none said anything mean or sarcastic. A few even said hey or hi.

Jackie was relieved that they'd had to be there early in order for Chris to take up his post at the door. She never did actually formulate the thought in her mind, "I don't want to be seen walking in with Chris." She didn't even know the thought was there. And they weren't seen together, at least not by Courtney or Erica or any of their friends. Chris was busy with the tickets and didn't notice when she slipped away.

Her stomach felt like she had taken it on the scariest roller-coaster ride ever when she saw Carter Leavitt — even though she had known, or at least hoped, that he would be there. She hadn't told anyone, certainly not Courtney, how she felt about Carter. She didn't have words to tell anyone how she felt about Carter. What was she to say — I feel funny when he stands close to me? But Courtney always seemed to know these things — who people liked and who liked them back. Jackie had said nothing to her, but Courtney had hinted that things happened at dances.

The Alpha and the Beta and the rest of the she-wolf pack jumped around and danced with each other, behaving especially giddily to songs they liked that were familiar from the radio. Jackie was much too self-conscious to join in. She felt both that everyone in the room was looking at, thinking, and talking about her, and that she was totally invisible and completely insignificant in the lives of everyone in attendance. She wandered over to the table where the DJs had set up and stood there.

Even after the flurry at the door died down, Chris continued to almost, sort of, halfway enjoy himself. He sat watching the others leap about, and noted to himself how, if he squinted his eyes, especially when the strobe light was on, the dancers looked like dolls and puppets. An adult chaperone, a woman who had been checking ID at the main door outside, came over and smiled at him.

"I can take over here now," she said. "Go have some fun."

A moment before, Chris wouldn't have believed he would say yes to her offer. But dolls and puppets were not so scary. He gave her his pile of tickets and left his post. Jackie was standing near the DJs' table and he walked toward her, but before he reached her, he saw Courtney and Erica each grab her by an arm and drag her into their circle on the dance floor. Jackie was resisting them, trying to pull back, but she was laughing at the same time. Carter Leavitt got hold of her as well, and then she was jumping and leaping with the rest of them.

Chris went to the concession and bought two cans of pop. He waited a long time, and finally the music slowed and the dolls and puppets stopped jumping. Whereas before no one was dancing with anyone in particular, something different began to happen now. People who liked people, trying to look casual, but hurrying at the same time, sauntered over to the people they liked. Chris went to Jackie and held out one of the cans.

"I got this for you," he said.

"Oh." She looked surprised and didn't take it.

"Do you want to dance?" he asked.

Jackie felt something like panic. "You're being a creep," she thought to herself, but thinking that didn't quell the panic. She saw Courtney looking at them. She couldn't slow dance with Chris.

"Sure," she said. "I have to go to the bathroom first, though."

"Okay," Chris said.

Jackie ducked away and left the room and Chris stood waiting for her. People were dancing to the slow song, holding each other both tightly and awkwardly, and he smiled to himself. He and Jackie and Sidney often laughed

about people their age slow dancing. They all looked very funny. He saw that Courtney Strachan-Smith was dancing with Carter Leavitt.

He stood for a long time, holding Jackie's pop and sipping from his own. The slow song ended, the fast music started up again, and people resumed jumping.

Jackie did not return.

He set her pop on the DJs' table and left the hall.

Jackie sat on the edge of the sink in the bathroom, waiting for the slow song to end. Maybe she could dance with Chris on the other side of the room, to a fast song. Maybe she could pull him into the circle of dancers, as had been done to her. Maybe she could walk home. Maybe she could walk to the moon. Maybe the floor would open and swallow her.

When Jackie emerged much later, many fast songs had passed and another slow one had begun. The lights in the bathroom were bright and the dance room was dark, and it took her eyes some time to adjust. Starr, who was crying in a corner, was being comforted by Jana. Jackie didn't see Chris anywhere. Courtney was dancing with Carter.

She was relieved when it was time for the Gummy to end. She'd had enough of leaping about in the circle, pretending to have fun, and standing on the sidelines during the slow dances, pretending that was fun too.

She hadn't worn a jacket, so she didn't have to fight her

way through the coatroom. She went outside and looked around for Chris. There was no sign of him on the steps; and he wasn't on the lawn below. She could see his father's car and ran down quickly. She pulled open the back door and slid in, and realized Chris wasn't there either.

Bob turned to her. "Where's Chris?" he asked.

"I didn't see him inside. I thought he was out here."

"Okay," Bob said. "How was the dance?"

"Good."

They waited in silence as kids streamed out of the community centre, shouting and laughing and climbing into their parents' cars. The silence between Jackie and Bob grew uncomfortable.

"Maybe he had to do something with the tickets," Jackie finally offered. "I'll go look for him."

"No, I'll go." Bob shut off the motor and slipped out from behind the steering wheel.

As Jackie sat slumped in the back seat, Courtney, Erica, Carter, Starr, Jana, Lindsay, William, and company streamed by. She surmised they were walking home, because Erica was smoking – something she probably wouldn't do if she were expecting her mother to pull up at any minute. Jackie slouched even lower in the seat and thought about what it would be like if she never had to see any of them again.

She could see Bob standing at the top of the steps,

talking to a chaperone.

He returned, without Chris, and got back in the car. "She said he left at ten o'clock."

Jackie responded in a small voice. "Oh."

"He didn't say anything to you?"

"No."

Bob sat, hands clenching the steering wheel. He muttered to himself, "Something must have happened," then turned again to Jackie. "Did something happen?"

"I don't know." She felt small. Small in heart.

She made herself look at Bob, whose brow was furrowed. He started the car, and she thought she heard him say, to himself again, "I shouldn't have let him come."

She wondered if he was thinking about Lindy.

BOB DROVE JACKIE HOME and ran up the sidewalk without even closing the car door.

"Chris is missing," he said to Mary as she opened the door to his ring. "I'm gonna run home and see if he's there, then I'll...." He stopped. "Call the police I guess."

He hurried back down the sidewalk to his car, and nodded without turning around when Mary shouted after him, "Call as soon as you get there, let me know."

She closed and locked the door and turned to Jackie anxiously.

"What happened?"

"I'm not sure.... He left early, I guess."

"What do you mean?" Mary asked.

"What do you mean?" was the same question Chris had asked, bewildered, when the policewoman told him his mother had died. That was what Jackie had thought about during Lindy's funeral. What do you mean, what do I mean, what do we mean? She thought about Chris jumping into the Kananaskis River to save his mother.

Jackie went to her room to wait. They lived nearby. Bob would call and say whether Chris was lost or found.

Chris was in his bedroom, sitting on the edge of the bed, when he heard his father come in the house, shouting, "Son?" He quickly picked up a book and arranged himself to look comfortable against the pillows, before calling out, "I'm in here."

Bob rushed in.

"Are you all right?"

"Yes."

"What happened?"

"Nothing."

Bob waited, but Chris didn't continue.

"Were those fools bothering you?"

The "fools" were the boys at school, who often either bothered Chris or didn't bother with him.

"No. It just wasn't my kind of thing, I guess, Dad. I didn't mean to scare you."

"You did though. You did scare me. You should have called if you wanted to come home early."

"I just felt like going for a walk."

They sat in silence for a few moments. Chris didn't like to see the sadness on his father's face, so he picked up his book and pretended to read.

"Okay, son," Bob said at last. "Good night."

"Good night."

Bob left the room and closed the door and Chris set down his book. He looked around his room, at his things. His various collections of rocks and seeds and twigs and vials and books. He saw himself in the mirror over his chest of drawers and stopped to ask himself a question.

"What's wrong with me?"

JACKIE HEARD the ringing of the telephone, and then Mary came and stood in her bedroom doorway.

"Chris is home. He went for a walk in the ravine."

"Oh. That's good." Jackie had twisted her hair tightly around her fingers, and now she let it go.

"Are you sure nothing happened?"

"Yes."

"Okay, good night then."

"Night."

As soon as the door closed, Jackie reached up and switched off her lamp. She wanted to lie in the dark and not see herself in the mirror.

CHAPTER 13

"H E'S NOT HERE RIGHT NOW. IT'S ME. HAFTA GET *your shoe off your foot, okay? It's all swollen."*

Sidney was shouting to be heard above the rain and wind. She shone the beam in Jackie's face. Jackie moaned and tried to turn her head away from the light.

She croaked something that sounded like "Pie good warts."

Sidney would have laughed if she hadn't been so surprised and relieved to hear Jackie talking. She directed the light away from Jackie's eyes.

"My foot hurts," Jackie said, more distinctly this time. "I'm cold."

"I know." Sidney turned the light's glow back to Jackie's foot. "I have to get this shoe off. Hold still if you can."

Sidney gently reapplied the blade of her knife to the laces and slowly sawed back and forth until they gave way. She opened the flaps and pulled the tongue forward, glancing at Jackie all the while.

"Is it hurting?" she asked. "I guess you wouldn't be wincing if it wasn't, huh? Hang on, I've almost got it."

She turned back to the shoe with her knife and made a slit through the canvas. Finally, it fell away and came free. Even through the sock, she could tell there was something very wrong with Jackie's ankle. It was swollen to three times its usual size.

Sidney took stock of their situation. They couldn't stay where they were. The wind was whipping her hair and chilling her wet skin through to her bones. But Jackie would not be able to walk, and Sidney doubted that she could carry her. Still, to stay where they were, with no shelter and nothing to hold onto but this tiny little bush, would be deadly. Sidney wished there was someone to help, someone to tell her what to do. But no one was coming — not in this storm, not tonight.

Jackie had reached out and taken her hand, but Sidney was afraid she was slipping away again. She wasn't talking.

"Jackie," she said, "I have to go find somewhere we can get out of this rain. We can't stay here. I'm going, but just for a minute...."

Jackie squeezed her hand, pleading. "Don't leave me. Don't, Sidney, no."

"Okay, okay." Sidney tried to undo the knot on the rope tied around her waist, but it was too wet and her fingers were too cold. She needed to warm up, to think. She had to make do with where they were for now. She crawled under the jacket and blanket, pulled the jacket over their heads, and wrapped her arms around her sister.

She thought she'd never been this wet before.

And then she remembered, and said to herself, "Oh, yes, I was."

BUT IT WAS A VERY LONG TIME AGO and far away from the side of this mountain.

The long-ago days when Sidney's life was perfect.

"Where are the other kids?"

Sidney had been helping her mother and Lindy pack up an enormous picnic lunch for the "halfventure" (Earl's word) they were taking that day.

"I think they went out in the backyard," Sidney responded, as she sliced the last of the strawberries and plunked them into the plastic container alongside the oranges.

"We're just about ready to go. Can you tell them to grab their jackets? You too."

Sidney was right. She found Jackie and Chris in the yard. Jackie was walking along the edge of the fence and

Chris was sitting on the grass below, trying to keep aloft three colourful balls from the juggling kit Jackie had given him for his birthday. Sidney stood and watched them for awhile, without their taking notice that she was there.

There was something in the way they were together. Sidney couldn't name it, but watching them there in their private moment filled her with a kind of longing for which she had no words. They were friends, they were more than friends. Like brother and sister, but that wasn't quite it either.

"Did you see it?" Chris was asking.

"Yeah. It was so lame."

They were discussing a counterfeit ten-dollar bill that Carter Leavitt's friend William Beach had made.

"He might as well have written the number ten on a gum wrapper."

"Yeah," Jackie replied. "In crayon."

Chris laughed and affected an idiot's voice. "This is legal tender."

William Beach was often in trouble. Sidney had once overheard her mother telling her father that she thought William would have a long and colourful career as a criminal. His plan had been to counterfeit his ten-dollar bills and sell them to his classmates for five dollars each.

"You make a profit, get it?" He had tried very hard to

persuade them. "You pay me five bucks, but then you get to buy ten bucks worth of stuff."

No one fell for it. Even the most gullible among them could see what a poor job he'd done of copying the bills.

"Those guys are so stupid," Chris continued, referring to William and his friends. Jackie carefully placed one foot in front of the other along the fence railing.

"Carter's not stupid," she said.

"You're not exactly a rocket scientist if William Beach is your best friend."

Jackie shrugged.

"Hey, look, look, I got it!" Chris called out excitedly. He had the balls spinning in the air in perfect sync.

Jackie teetered, lost her balance, and jumped to the ground beside Chris. She laughed. Chris juggled. Sidney watched a moment longer.

Then, "Guys," she said from the corner of the yard, "You're supposed to get your jackets."

THE PLACE WHERE EARL AND BOB inflated the raft was at the bottom of a smooth pathway, just above a small inlet the river had sculpted out of the earth. Sidney wanted to help, but her legs and arms weren't strong enough to operate the pumps, so she contented herself by bossing everyone else. She directed Bob and Earl in the use of the pump, gave advice to Chris and Jackie on rock skipping, and prompted Mary and Lindy in the placement of their feet in the raft when they were finally ready to push off.

"Bob, you'll have to do most of the steering, since you're the only one who's done this river before. Daddy can help you though. Uhhm, let me see. I guess, Chris, you and Jackie should take the front paddles."

They did so, after licking their red, sticky fingers. In addition to throwing rocks, they had been picking and eating wild strawberries.

Strawberries were Sidney's favourite wild berry. There was nothing else that looked like a strawberry, and nothing else that tasted as good. When they were learning how to identify edible berries in Junior Forest Wardens, and how to avoid poisonous ones, Sidney had had a terrible time telling the difference between buffalo berries and chokecherries, and bearberries from bog cranberries, until Jackie had pointed out to her that you had to look at the whole plant – the bark, the leaves, the size of the tree or bush. But even now, after Sidney had studied and pored over pictures and wandered for hours through meadows and forests, looking at bushes and berries and shrubs until she was the best in the club, she still thought of the strawberry as the one that fairy mothers fed to their curly-haired fairy children. Wild strawberries were part of Sidney's magical world.

Chris knew this, and he dropped several fat ones onto

Sidney's outstretched palm. She immediately popped them into her mouth, oblivious to the fact that Chris had just been licking his fingers.

While Sidney's mouth was full and she was unable to argue, Bob decided the weight had to be distributed more evenly on the raft, for the sake of balance. He had the three children and the women trade places, as he and Earl held onto ropes. Mary wobbled.

"You sure this thing is gonna hold us all, Robert?" she asked Chris's father.

"Yes," Bob answered, as he and Earl gave the raft a little push away from the riverbank, then tumbled into the back.

"Everybody's all zipped, right?" Mary anxiously looked around, checking their life jackets.

"Yes, Mother, everybody's zipped," Jackie and Sidney answered in unison.

They encountered few rapids at first, which turned out to be a good thing. Both Mary and Lindy were so inept at their job of paddling, that the first twenty minutes of the river-rafting trip was spent careening from one side of the river to the other, while making very little forward progress. The women had trouble coordinating their paddles. They couldn't master the art of digging in at the right time, at least not both of them at once.

At one point, as the raft sailed straight for a bed of

sharp rocks that threatened to ground them, Lindy decided enough was enough. She stood up, wearing a very determined expression, her tongue sticking out from the corner of her mouth. Leaning over dangerously far, she planted her paddle amidst the offending rocks and gave a shove. The force of the push sent the raft spinning around and around in the middle of the river, causing Lindy to lose her balance.

"Ahhh!" she yelped, her arms flailing about in the air. As she rocked backwards, she tried to steady herself by grabbing a handful of Chris's hair, and then smacked Mary in the face with her bum. Sidney laughed so hard she fell over on her side.

Bob and Earl fought against the spin with their paddles, at last managing to steady the raft.

Chris rubbed his head.

"Ow, Mom, it's a raft ride, not breakdancing!"

By this time, Lindy had regained her dignity and found her place next to Mary.

"Are you okay, honey?" Bob asked, chuckling.

"I'm sorry," she said.

Chris looked at Sidney, who remained on her side laughing, then turned to Jackie.

"What's the matter with her?"

Jackie rolled her eyes. "Bum in face? Don't you know anything to do with bums is hysterically funny?" she responded with a small sigh.

Bob admitted that Sidney's plan was best, after all. Once more he rearranged the passengers so that Jackie and Chris handled the front paddles and Mary and Lindy took their places in the middle, next to Sidney.

Thus settled, they continued on their way.

The Kananaskis River rolled along, carrying them effortlessly, as there had been a lot of snow the previous winter and the water was deep and fast. Bob told them it would be like this, relatively calm and easy, for the first twenty minutes or so, and that their halfventure lay further downstream. He said this was a "class 3" rapids, not exactly for beginners, but certainly not dangerous and thrilling, like a "class 5" river would have been. It was green and clear, and Sidney wished both to look over the edge of the raft, to see the smooth rocks lying on the riverbed, and to look up, so as not to miss any details of the cliffs and hills that rose above them on either side. In the end, she settled for trailing a hand in the water as she looked above – the rocks below were only rocks, after all, and after a time seemed to look more or less the same. What was above changed all the time. At one point the clouds resembled Pegasus, the winged horse. Hawks and ravens soared far overhead, the hawks swooping and silent, the ravens swift and calling harshly, not caring who heard them. Sidney spotted both a coyote and a fawn, and even though she understood that coyotes had to eat, just like everyone else, she hoped that particular fawn would not become that particular coyote's dinner. When they drifted near the river's edge, Sidney could reach up and touch the branches of trees that overhung the water. It was remarkable to her the way some of the trees did not grow straight up at all, but instead grew vertically out of the side of a hill, the roots visible, trying to hang on, like an older child trying to prevent her younger brother from falling into the water.

"Daddy," she called out, above the rush of the river, "Will that tree fall in someday?"

"I suppose it might. If enough of the soil eroded and the roots had nothing to grip."

"Then what?"

"It would float until it snagged on something, I guess, or...."

"Here we go, everybody!" Bob interrupted them.

"What?" Mary asked.

"Hear that roaring? That's the rapids."

"I guess that means we're about to begin our halfventure," Lindy said to Mary.

Sure enough, they could see ahead of them a churning white froth, a place where the river jumped.

"Okay, what do we do?" Mary asked nervously.

"We don't do anything, right, Robert?" Lindy asked her husband.

"You just hold on. Jackie and Chris have done this before."

The raft began to tip and buck, as the water beneath grew agitated.

"All right, paddle everyone!" Bob shouted, and the four paddlers leaned into their task, rowing furiously. "Left, left, left, Chris! Let's go!"

The rapids tossed the front of the raft into the air, then smacked it down once again, sending a great spray of water washing over Jackie and Chris.

"AAaah!" they both screamed, shocked by their cold dousing. They laughed and paddled all the more furiously.

The raft pitched and rocked and was tossed around, and then they were through and once again sailing along with the calm current. Mary and Lindy both loosened the grip they'd had on the raft's handles.

"That was great!" Earl crowed.

"It wasn't so bad, hey Lind?" Mary said to her friend. "But I don't understand, Bob. Why were you telling Chris to paddle left? You took us right into the middle of the worst part. If we'd gone right, we could have avoided that mess."

Everyone stared at her, then Jackie burst out laughing. "The point is to go into the rapids, Mom. That's what we were trying to do, that's the fun of it."

"Oh. I thought.... Oh well," she said brightly. "It

wasn't so bad really. If that's all there is to it, we survived and that's that."

The others, with the exception of Lindy, laughed again. Mary shot Lindy a questioning look.

"I think that means there are more rapids," Lindy dryly explained.

"Yep, like right up there." Sidney pointed.

Mary muttered, "If this is a halfventure, I'd hate to see a whole one." They continued along the river at such a pace that she didn't have time to worry. She became more confident with each rapids conquered. The raft rose and fell, spun, and even threatened to tip, but Mary and Lindy and everyone else hung on, laughing and shouting exuberantly when the cold Kananaskis River splashed their faces and soaked their life jackets.

The two women grew brave enough that they wanted to take a turn at the front paddles again. Bob was hesitant, warning them that there was a small waterfall ahead, which would provide their greatest challenge, but Lindy and Mary argued that the only way for them to become better paddlers for future trips was to try again. Bob agreed, so Jackie and Chris carefully switched places with their mothers, directed by Sidney. This time it took Mary and Lindy only a few seconds to master their paddles and each congratulated the other on her skill.

And everything probably would have been fine, if it

hadn't been for the heavier than usual snowfall the Kananaskis had received the previous winter. None of them knew that the little waterfall that usually provided a thrill for the river's riders was now proving to be a hazard, even for experienced rafters. With the exception of Bob, none of them could be called experienced.

He knew as soon as he heard the roar ahead that something was different this time. The river was flowing swiftly enough that, within moments of hearing the falls, they were nearly upon them and could see the angry boil of the water.

"Uh-oh," Bob said quietly, but he knew there was nothing to be done, there was no turning back and they were travelling much too fast to try to fight the current and make for the riverbank.

"Hang on everybody!" was all he had time to shout.

Twice they were in danger of being spilled from the raft – the first time when they shot over the rim, and the second as the nose of the raft dipped and the rear of the raft was pushed up by the force of the water and almost flipped over. Somehow, although jostled and tossed, everyone hung on as the water rocked them this way and that and then they were almost through, the worst was over, they would have been laughing and cocky again from the relief and the exhilaration, except Lindy had her eyes closed and when she opened them she saw herself spinning toward one of those overhanging trees. By reflex, she lifted her paddle to protect herself – it snapped upward and caught a heavy branch. The speed at which they were moving, and the branch catching the paddle as it did, lifted Lindy out of the raft and tossed her into the water.

She immediately disappeared under the raft, and before his father could stop him, Chris dived into the river after her. It all happened so quickly. As Bob was slipping his shoes off and preparing to dive in as well, the bright orange of Chris and Lindy's life jackets bobbed up ahead of the raft.

Sidney spotted them first.

"There they are!" she cried, and snatched the paddle from her mother's hand, leaning into it for all she was worth, as Bob and her father did the same. They paddled toward the bobbing figures ahead and hauled them, slippery and dripping, into the raft.

The strange thing was when Sidney remembered that day later on, she couldn't recall the details of those scary moments, or even being scared at all. She knew she had been afraid, because Jackie reminded her later that when Lindy first fell in, Sidney had screamed, grabbed Jackie's sleeve, and bitten down on it.

The only thing she could recall very clearly was the look on Chris's face when his mother disappeared.

What she remembered about the rest of the day was

how warm it felt, and that once they had everyone safely back in the raft, they floated downstream until they came to a place where they could have gone left or right, because the water parted to make way for an island. And how they decided not to go either way, but to pull up on the little island to eat their lunch. Despite all the splashing and dousing, the big orange waterproof bag had done its job and the lunches were intact.

Mary was quiet for the rest of the day. She was the only one who couldn't seem to shake off that one small moment of terror they'd all shared, when they thought Lindy was gone. Lindy laughed and hugged Mary tight before she took off her sodden shoes and socks and laid them out in the sun.

"I'm okay," she said. "I really am."

That's what Sidney remembered. How much they all loved each other as they stretched out on their private little island and admired the geometric shapes she had formed from the strawberries and oranges. Life was perfect then.

CHAPTER 14

J ACKIE AWOKE TO FIND SHE WAS ALONE.

For the first time since she'd felt her ankle twist and the wrenching pain had sent her tumbling down the slope, she wondered if it would be better not to wake again. Because waking into pain was one thing, as she had been doing. But waking alone, when she had thought Sidney was there, left her feeling completely hopeless. In much pain, and barely able to hold onto consciousness, Jackie was unable to connect Sidney's blanket and raincoat and backpack under her head to the fact that Sidney had really been there, and would come back. She was miserable.

Jackie had thought from time to time over the past year that she knew the meaning of the word misery, because she believed she had experienced it. She'd thought she was miserable the day she wore her new shoes to school and, from the corner of her eye, she'd caught the briefest glance passing between Courtney and Erica. The tiniest moment, barely measurable – Courtney had glanced at Jackie's shoes and then flashed a look at Erica, and the corner of Erica's mouth had twitched up into that sneering smile she always wore, and Jackie knew in that moment she could never wear those shoes again.

Her mother was bewildered. She'd had to argue with Earl to allow Jackie to spend seventy-eight dollars on a pair of shoes, and now Jackie had placed them in the back of the closet and was refusing to wear them. She was bewildered and then angry, and wondered why, and Jackie couldn't tell her. Even then, Jackie knew she was being stupid and shallow and foolish, but she couldn't make herself put those shoes on again, and she couldn't tell her mother why. Feeling stupid in that way, she thought was misery.

She thought differently now. Being here, in the rain, on the mountain, dreaming that Sidney had come, and then waking up and realizing she hadn't been there, that was misery. Knowing it was her own fault, that was misery. Hurting Chris. Hurting Chris.

JACKIE WAS TEACHING CHRIS how to pass a soccer ball in the park the day of Lindy's car accident.

Chris had not been doing well in the soccer unit in

phys. ed., so they worked on passing and dribbling for an hour or so, until they got thirsty and went to the big old stone fountain next to the swings for a drink. Chris was in a silly mood. He took a mouthful of water and let some of it run out of his mouth onto the ground. It splashed Jackie's runners.

"Ew." She gave him a little shove. "What are you doing?"

"Dribbling," he answered.

She took a mouthful and spewed the entire amount onto Chris's shirt.

Chris bent to the fountain and filled his mouth and cheeks until they were puffed out to the limits. Jackie had already started running by then. Chris gave chase, but they both knew he wouldn't catch her. They ran laughing and laughing and laughing all the way to Jackie's house. When they got there, a police car was parked outside and Jackie's father gravely met them at the door.

The accident was reported in the news for several weeks, because the driver of the truck ahead of Lindy hadn't properly secured the load of pipes he was carrying. One of them slipped off and smashed through Lindy's windshield, and the driver was charged with negligence. The newspapers ran articles with headlines like "Driver Sorry for Freak Occurrence" underneath a photograph of Lindy's smiling face. Bob cancelled his subscriptions to the newspapers.

CHAPTER 15

THE CRASHING OF THE THUNDER AND ERUPTIONS OF *lightning over her head seemed like explosions going off all around Jackie.*

She was frightened of her thoughts. It was scary to wonder if it would be better not to wake again. It was hopeless to think of escaping from the mountain. It was almost hopeless to think that someone would find her. There was something else, too. That question – how did I get here?

She forced herself to put that thought away and tried to think of better things. She thought of her family and how they loved her and how she loved them. She thought of Papa Williams in the blue suit he wore every Sunday.

"PAPA," she had said to him one Sunday morning as he

polished his shoes, "don't you get tired of wearing that same suit?"

"Nope."

"Why not?"

"It's my church suit."

"Yes, but...don't people at your church get tired of it?"

"Nope."

"How do you know?"

"They love me as me, y'see? They don't see my suit. They see me."

Jackie wasn't sure about this. She loved Papa too, yet still wished he would wear a different suit to church sometimes. But if Papa wanted to think no one noticed, that was all right with her.

She loved Nana and Papa's church and looked forward to going along with them on the occasions when she and Sidney spent weekends at their house. Quite often, Grandpa Bailey and the members of his former band would bring their instruments and accompany the choir or play and sing special songs, and when they did, Jackie thought they might blow the church roof from over their heads. Sitting next to Papa, Jackie would watch his foot tap up and down in time with the music and hear him say quietly to himself, "Yesss, uhhm hmm, yes, brother."

Driving home from church was good too. Nana and Sidney would ride in the back seat, always determined to stay awake, but the sun streaming in through the window would defeat them. Jackie rode up front with Papa.

One Sunday she told him she liked his church better than any other.

"I feel normal there," she said.

"What you mean by that?"

"I dunno. I went to church with my friend one time and it felt really strange. Everybody was the same colour."

Papa looked at her. "Church is the last place you should be thinkin that, baby girl."

"Why?"

"It's like with my suit, y'see? You oughta look at the person, not the costume. Not the shell."

Jackie shrugged. "I just feel like I fit in there, that's all."

Many of the people who attended Papa's church were Black; some whose families had lived in Alberta for almost one hundred years, like Papa's, and some from Africa and the Caribbean. There were three families from the nearest reserve. Some of the people were Chinese. Many, many of the children were like Jackie and Sidney – having parents of different races or cultural backgrounds. The pastor once joked that he was going to change the name of the church to "Heinz 57." Jackie asked Papa what he meant by that, and he explained that Pastor Brown was referring to a sauce made with fifty-seven different spices.

"Now, tell me somethin'," Papa said. "How can a person be normal one place and not normal someplace else?"

"I dunno. Ask your daughter."

Jackie and Papa often puzzled over Mary together. They shared a little joke – if Mary did something perplexing, Papa would say, "That's your mother," and Jackie would reply, "That's your daughter."

"She knows all about that, does she?"

"Guess so. She's always telling me and Sidney to be normal."

Papa's voice dropped. "No she doesn't, baby girl."

"Well, maybe not exactly in those words. But that's what she means."

Papa took his eyes off the road for a moment to look at her with his eyes that were so brown they were almost black. Jackie leaned over and turned up the music on the CD player. The woman singing had a strange sounding voice, low and quavery, like Grandpa Bailey's saxophone. Jackie liked it.

"What's this song about, Papa?"

The trembly voiced woman sang these words.

I don't know nothin 'bout it
I don't care nothin 'bout it
I have been in danger

98

I've only known a stranger
Why don't I know nothin 'bout havin been in danger?
I've only known a stranger, a stranger, a stranger
Oh, in danger

"What you think it's about?" Papa asked back.

Jackie thought for a few minutes. "Maybe it's about how you feel scared when you think you know someone, but then they do something you didn't think they would do."

Papa nodded. "Could be. Or maybe it's about the things we do to ourselves. Nothin's more dangerous than forgettin who we are."

They rode along in silence for a little while.

"You know, baby, your mother doesn't think there's anything wrong with you girls. She thinks there's somethin wrong with the world. She wants you to be strong. She doesn't want you to be hurt."

"What does she think is gonna hurt us?"

"Hateful people. Ignorant people."

"Oh."

Jackie hit the repeat button and listened to the song again.

CHAPTER 16

"How did I get here? How did this happen to me?" *Jackie wanted to see her Papa again.*

She wanted to tell him he was right about the song.

She wanted Sidney.

Jackie's mind felt more clear when she tried to focus on people she loved. It was as though strength from them reached through the fog that surrounded her thoughts. Her hand wandered to something that covered her. Was it a blanket? A coat? Who had covered her? She found a pocket — and there was a feather in it. She closed her hand around it.

She wanted to say something to Chris.

She remembered watching him on the podium at Lindy's funeral, listening to the poem he read, and thinking he was the strongest person in the world, to want to say goodbye to his mom in that way. Chris had insisted on reading, against

Bob's wishes. His voice was quiet but didn't shake. He didn't cry.

Jackie recalled reaching out to hold his hand when he returned to his place next to her, and finding that he was clutching his favourite stone from his rock collection. It was the stone he and Lindy had found together on the little island where they ate their lunch after the infamous halfventure. She remembered being the girl who didn't mind that Chris's hand was sweaty from clutching the rock. She remembered being that girl. She had known her very well. But this girl she had become, Jackie didn't know her. She was a stranger.

As THE TIME for the end-of-year camping trip drew near, Jackie began to dread it more as each second passed. Up to three weeks before, she had been growing more confident of her place within Courtney's circle of friends. It seemed that she was one of them. Unfortunately, she found their conversation dull and was often embarrassed by the way they behaved toward Mrs. Waldren at school.

She began to notice something she hadn't realized from outside of Courtney's circle. Mrs. Waldren was afraid of Courtney. The less respect Courtney showed her, the more Mrs. Waldren allowed Courtney to do whatever she liked. It was as though they had made a bargain.

Courtney's friends did as Courtney chose to lead them. Mrs. Waldren would pretend she found their antics amusing, that she was allowing it because she was cool. But Jackie could see that behind Mrs. Waldren's tight smile was a woman in fear of losing control. Courtney would sense when Mrs. Waldren was about to break, and just as suddenly as Courtney's friends had turned the temperature up on whatever activity they fancied that particular day, Courtney would have them shut it off. They would turn back into children, and Mrs. Waldren would be grateful to Courtney. She would allow herself to pretend she had regained control of the classroom. She would smile at Courtney, and Courtney would smile sweetly back.

Jackie learned how to participate in these class rumbles. She would catch Chris looking at her, and she would feel ashamed and shallow, but she would turn away. Jackie became more and more accepted by the alpha and her betas, but Chris stopped respecting her, and then it seemed he stopped liking her.

The first time Jackie saw Chris after the community centre dance was at school the following Monday. She had spent the entire weekend thinking about what she would say when she saw him. She had a plan.

Chris was already in the coatroom when she arrived, hanging his blue jacket on its hook and taking books from his backpack. Jackie's hook was next to his, so getting close to him was easy enough. She took a deep breath, slipped out of her own jacket, and slid over to where Chris was standing.

"Hey," she said, breezily.

Chris didn't answer, or look at her.

"What happened to you Friday night?" she went on. "I wasn't feeling good and I was in the bathroom a long time, and then when I came out, you...."

Chris cut her off. "Don't talk to me like I'm stupid, Jackie."

"What?" she stammered.

He walked away, into the classroom, and sat down at his desk.

Jackie followed him. "Chris."

"That's right. It's me, Chris. I'm not one of your tiny-brained new friends."

He took out a book and started reading. Jackie stood a few moments longer, her face hot, then turned and walked over to her own desk across the room.

Later that day, during Chris's oral report on geysers, Courtney and Erica began to giggle and chat.

Chris stopped talking. There was a coldness around his eyes.

"Excuse me," he said.

Everyone else in the classroom became quiet, except

for Courtney and Erica, who hadn't heard him.

"Excuse me," he said again, and this time they looked up at him.

"I wasn't finished." His voice was as cold as his eyes.

Courtney laughed, and so did some others. Some didn't.

Chris continued to stare at Courtney.

"Let's carry on, shall we, Chris?" Mrs. Waldren said nervously. "Chris is reminding us of our code of conduct, isn't he, class? We want to show respect for one another."

"Oh yes. Sorry," Courtney said sweetly. The only person in the room who bought Courtney's sweet smile was Mrs. Waldren. Everyone else knew what the look in Courtney's eyes meant. "I'll get you," it meant.

Courtney did get Chris, many times, or so she thought. But something had happened to him. He had stopped believing there was anything he could do to find acceptance at school. He had stopped thinking, "If only I do this, if only I do that, I'll have friends." He had stopped trying not to care. Courtney's plots and tricks and meanness were wasted on him.

It made him powerful in a lonely, noble sort of way.

Jackie no longer had the option of turning to Chris when all else failed. She now had to rely entirely on Courtney's moods to ensure that she didn't eat alone at lunchtime, sit alone on the bus, walk around alone at recess. She had to work harder than ever to make sure she did everything right, to make sure Courtney didn't turn on her. And things fell into place. Everything was good.

Until the day Courtney didn't like her shoes. Then everything went bad.

CHAPTER 17

SIDNEY WAS NOT FAR AWAY, EVEN AT THE MOMENT WHEN *Jackie was wishing for her.*

She had stayed with Jackie, doing her best to keep her warm, because she knew very well that the bad weather was their enemy. Jackie was injured, as well as cold and wet, and possibly in shock.

She had never before been in a position where she had to decide things for Jackie. Jackie was better than she was at everything, except Forest Wardens, and that was only because Jackie had quit. But her number one, usual option – to ask Jackie for advice – was not open in this instance. None of her usual options were available, she realized. Her parents weren't there, nor her grandparents, nor Chris, nor Kate. She felt a little angry with all of them. She felt let down and alone. What was she doing out there all by her-

self? She felt especially angry at Gala. Where was the magic in this?

She lay there for what seemed like a long time, arms around Jackie, as the rain drummed her ears under the blanket and the thunder roared, sometimes nearby, sometimes far away. Her anger ebbed away, replaced by fear, and then the fear was replaced with resolve.

She didn't want to leave Jackie alone, because Jackie had asked her not to. But she knew she had to find a better place for them to wait out this storm.

She tucked her backpack beneath Jackie's head, as a sign that she would come back, in case Jackie woke up, slipped the raincoat and blanket securely around Jackie's body, and crept away.

Without the protection of the covers and the warmth of Jackie's body, the shock of the wind and rain hit Sidney full force. She clamped her teeth together to keep them from chattering, gripped her flashlight and, shining the beam before her, crawled away from Jackie's tree.

It was only then she remembered her rope was still tied around her waist. It certainly wasn't long enough to allow her to go much farther. She tried the knot again, but her fingers were very stiff. She flexed and rubbed and blew on them, but nothing helped. "Stupids!" she said, frustration washing over her. She gripped her knife and found that her fingers at least worked well enough to flip open the blade and cut the rope.

She looked at the rope as it lay slack on the ground. "I'm going to need it."

There it might lie forever, as far as she knew, and that would be useless. There could be a hundred ways for it to be helpful before she and Jackie found their way out of this mess. She thought about pulling herself back up to Brid's tree, untying it, and then trying to get back down to Jackie. But she'd barely made it down, even with the rope. There was no way she could do it again without. In the end, she climbed up about three metres – as far as she dared. She cut the rope, reasoning that three metres was better than none, then crawled sideways on her hands and knees back down to Jackie's tree, and left the section of rope there.

Then, still on all fours, she moved carefully off to the right and in a slightly downward direction. She knew what she was doing was extremely dangerous and went very slowly, stopping frequently to swallow, to take a breath, to hold the flashlight up and peer through the darkness. She wasn't sure if it was just her own wishful thinking, but it seemed that the rain had slackened slightly.

Her instincts were leading her in the right direction, and before too long she found the slope of the mountain more gradual – enough to allow her to walk almost erect. She was starting to feel nervous about getting too far away from Jackie when she came to a place that would do. It was far from ideal – nothing more than a flattish ledge with an outcropping of *rock on one side and a scrawny little stand of trees nearby. That was about the best shelter she was going to find, and there they would be in less danger of sliding off the cliff.*

"Chris."

He jumped. "You scared me! What are you doing?"

He had just stepped out of the shower in the basement of his house, wrapped in a towel, and there was Sidney, lurking.

"Sorry. I didn't mean to. I just wanted to ask you something."

Chris padded in his bare feet across the hallway to his bedroom and went in, closing the door almost all the way.

"It's okay, I can hear you," he said through the tiny opening.

Sidney could hear him opening drawers.

"I'm just wondering why you've been so mean to Jackie."

She heard hangers slide across the bar in the closet. She heard rustling and the sound of socks being pulled over feet.

"Chris?"

He came out of his room, dressed.

"What's everyone doing?" he asked.

By everyone he meant Sidney's parents and his father. Jackie had stayed home.

"Playing cards," she answered.

"You wanna play Zolgarina?" he asked and sat down on the couch in the games room.

She stood where she was.

"'Cause when her friends leave her out at lunchtime and stuff, you never sit with her anymore. And you never come over, even when Mom...even when Jackie asks you."

Chris silently worked the controls of the game.

"Sometimes people just grow apart, I guess," he said flatly.

Sidney knew him well enough to understand that was all he had to say on the subject. She sat down next to him and picked up the other control. There was a time when she would have been thrilled to have Chris to herself, without having to compete with Jackie for his attention. She used to make up conversations she'd had with him to share with Gala and Ziggy – casual conversations like the ones he had with Jackie, where they laughed about people they knew who were silly.

But now that she did have Chris to herself, she just sat. She felt restless and listless all at the same time. She watched, without much interest, as boldly coloured, furtive figures flitted across the television screen, searching for the mask of Zolgarina. She was startled when the control slipped from her hand and fell to the floor.

She left Chris and went back upstairs, although she could hear the game of cribbage continuing and wasn't interested in that either. She sat on the steps and listened to her parents talking to Bob.

"Fifteen two, fifteen four, and a pair for six," her father said.

"I've got nothing." She heard the sound of Bob throwing down his cards.

"I don't know," said her mother. "I've tried talking with her, but she just says they're still friends."

Sidney heard the sound of cards being shuffled.

"Same with Chris. 'Nothing's wrong. Everything's fine, Dad, don't worry.'"

Sidney listened a while longer. Her parents had been having this same conversation for two weeks – what was wrong between Jackie and Chris? Should they send Jackie on the end-of-year school camping trip? Did she want to go? Was Chris going? Did he want to go?

Sidney could have guessed correctly if they'd asked her. Neither Chris nor Jackie wanted to go on the annual Division Two, end-of-year school camping trip. But it was unheard of not to go, especially for Grade Sixes.

Later that night when they returned home, Sidney went into Jackie's room to say good night, but Jackie appeared to be asleep. Hours after everyone in the house had gone to bed, Sidney was still awake. Her clock ticked. The springs in her mattress squeaked. A car on the street outside drove slowly past. All sounds that she wouldn't have noticed in the daytime, they were now ominous, and made her feel alone.

SIDNEY WAS MORE CONFUSED about what was happening to Jackie than she'd been about anything, ever. Her sister, who was good at everything, who never made mistakes, who never tripped over cracks in sidewalks, whose stomach never growled at the wrong time.

Whatever was happening to Jackie, including quitting Junior Forest Wardens, had a great deal to do with Courtney Strachan-Smith and Erica and their friends. And Carter Leavitt. Sidney saw those people every day. They went to the same school. But she couldn't penetrate their world or understand their codes.

Her world, as far as school went, was simple. She and Kate were best friends and that was more important than anything else. Sidney accepted that Kate's rings were necessary to the ordering of the universe and Kate never questioned Sidney's stories of magical encounters. They often found they were thinking of the same flavour of ice cream at the same time, and they both believed that boys were people, but not people in the usual sense. They picked their noses and, in general, Sidney believed, the less one had to do with them, the better. Except for Chris.

Jackie used to know that. Now, Sidney had to look on in disbelief as Jackie laughed at Carter Leavitt's antics. When Sidney pointed out to Jackie that Carter's greatest talent seemed to be his ability to belch "Silent Night," Jackie just shrugged and said that at least his belches didn't smell.

Jackie's relationships with the girls in her class were just as perplexing to Sidney as her sudden blindness to the many faults of the boys.

Who could make sense of being friends with people who were mean and made you cry?

Who could make sense of that?

WHEN SHE WAS MUCH YOUNGER, Sidney had come home from school frightened after a presentation on fire prevention. She was convinced Ziggy was planning to set a fire in her house. Ziggy was mischievous and had become so good at tricking people that her mother had told Sidney to stop blaming Ziggy for bad things that happened around the house. She was angry with Ziggy for fooling her mother into believing Sidney was the bad one, and had told Ziggy she couldn't come around anymore.

She didn't see her again after that, but she was frightened after the fire safety presentation. Ziggy was the sort who might set a fire. For several nights, she lay awake watching for her, which was difficult because she always found it easier to see invisible people with her eyes closed, but when she closed her eyes, she would start to fall asleep, and how could she make sure Ziggy couldn't set a fire if she was asleep?

Her mother had a long talk with her about how we all frighten ourselves with harmful worries and how important it is to face up to our fears. Her father called the school to say he thought the fire safety presentation was too graphic. Jackie asked her mother and father if she could sleep on the spare mattress in Sidney's room and they agreed.

"You can sleep there if you want," Sidney said to Jackie as she arranged her oversized pillow and her stuffed penguin on the spare mattress, "but I still have to watch for Ziggy."

"Okay," Jackie said. She snuggled underneath the quilt and yawned a big yawn. "Let's play a game to help us stay awake."

"Yeah! Say I'm the older sister this time, and you're my little sister and you caught measles, but I'm afraid to take you to the doctor because he might send us to the orphanage, so I...."

"No, it's too late to play that. Mom and Dad will get

mad if they hear us walking around. Let's just play a talking game. I'll think of something really big that I love you more than, then you think of something back."

"Okay," Sidney said.

"Okay. You know the beach near the hotel where we stayed in Bermuda?"

"Yeah."

"And you know the beach where Daddy built that alligator in the sand in Nova Scotia?"

"Yeah."

"And you know Long Beach, right?"

"Yeah."

"Well, if you took every grain of sand from those three beaches, then if you took every grain of sand from every beach on every shore in every country in the world and counted every single grain of sand, I love you more than that."

Sidney grinned. She could beat that. "Okay, you remember last winter when it snowed every day for three weeks straight?"

"Yes," Jackie said.

"And you know how it's snowed about two hundred times every winter that we've been alive?"

"Yeah."

"And you know how it snows in other cities and towns and countries everywhere?"

"Yeah."

"Well, if you took every snowflake that's ever fallen, in every part of the world, every single winter from when the world first started, and you counted them up and multiplied them by one gazillion, I love you more than that."

"Oh. That was a good one." Jackie thought for a moment. "Okay, what about this. You know our solar system, right?"

"Uhhm hmm."

"Well, say you took...."

Sidney interrupted her with a yawn.

"Jackie, I like this game but it's making me sleepy, and I have to stay awake because of Ziggy."

"Why don't I wait for her?" Jackie asked.

Sidney yawned again. "You don't even know what Ziggy looks like. You've never seen her."

"She's skinny, has dirty fingernails, and carries a red backpack."

Sidney stared at Jackie, amazed.

"I know all your friends, Nuthead. You've only told me about them eight million times. Anyway, it doesn't matter if I know what she looks like. She's not coming."

"How do you know?"

"She moved."

"As if."

"Remember when you told her she couldn't come around anymore? I followed her out of the house and she told me you were a little goody-goody that was no fun anymore anyway. She said she was moving to Norway."

"For real?"

"Yeah."

Sidney was quiet for so long Jackie thought she'd fallen asleep. But then her sleepy little voice asked, "Are you sure?"

"A gazillion percent."

"She said I was a goody-goody?"

"Yes."

Sidney was quiet for a time again, but then her even sleepier voice said, "I've got one, Jackie. You can't beat this one."

"What is it?"

"I love you more than everything that has a name."

CHAPTER 18

*S*IDNEY FOUND JACKIE JUST AS SHE'D LEFT HER. NOW *her only problem was how to get her sister to the sheltered spot. She thought maybe she could carry her. Jackie wasn't much bigger than Sidney and they often used to carry each other around playing the lonely orphans game. She bent low and tried to lift her, but Jackie felt like a sack of rocks. This wouldn't do. Piggybacking her sister around the house was one thing. Carrying her across a treacherous mountainside in the rain was another. She slid her arms out from underneath Jackie's still form.*

Jackie opened her eyes. She tried to focus on the large round object hovering over her. Was it Sidney? Yes, it was. She was very happy to see her.

She opened her mouth to speak and some words came out, but her voice was weak and the words were slurred.

What she tried to say was, "I thought you were a dream."

Sidney puzzled over what Jackie was trying to tell her, then nodded. "That's good," she replied. "I got you a new spleen too." She pushed her plastered-down hair out of her eyes for the millionth time, then knelt next to Jackie and continued. "Jackie, I have to move you. I know it's not good to do when someone's hurt, but if we don't get dry we're both gonna get hypothermia, right?"

Jackie mumbled.

"Jackie? You hafta stay awake now, for a little while, 'kay? You can move all your toes and fingers, right? Except for your hurt foot? Do you think your spine is okay, and your neck?...Jackie?"

Jackie closed her eyes again, but this time she wasn't drifting away, she was working very hard to come back. Sidney was really here and she was trying to help, and Jackie wanted to help too.

"Okay," she said. "I'll try to walk. Where are we going?"

"I don't think you can walk. I'm gonna drag you on the raincoat. But you hafta hang on really tight. Can you?"

Jackie nodded.

Sidney nodded too. She helped Jackie to sit up, very carefully, and slipped the raincoat underneath her. Then she wrapped the emergency blanket around Jackie and helped her uncurl her cramped, frigid fingers. She clasped her sister's hands between her own and vigorously rubbed until Jackie had regained feeling.

"Can you hold the flashlight?"

Jackie nodded.

Sidney gave her the light. "Hold on tight. Here we go."

She stuffed her piece of rope into her backpack, then took hold of the raincoat hood and cautiously inched her way along in the direction of the ledge. She had to be so careful. It seemed to take forever to cover a metre or two of ground. She finally reached the place where she could stand, and breathed a sigh of relief. The mountainside was slippery, which was a good thing for pulling your sister on a makeshift sled, but a bad thing for keeping your footing. Perhaps overconfident now that she could stand, and eager to get to safety, Sidney increased her pace. Her leg slid out from under her, and she crashed to the ground with a heavy thud.

"Sidney!" Jackie cried.

Sidney didn't answer.

"Sidney!"

Tears burning her eyes, Sidney clumsily got to her feet. "I'm okay."

More cautiously now, she continued.

Centimetre by tiny centimetre, they progressed.

"Shine the light up there, to my right," she said after a time.

Jackie did so and Sidney could see the little grove of trees. They were almost there. She stopped for a rest and looked back at Jackie, but couldn't see the expression on her face. Sidney went on.

"Here," she said at last.

She settled Jackie against the rocks and collapsed next to her, catching her breath. The raincoat was muddy, but otherwise had withstood the journey quite well.

"Here, put this back on," she said to Jackie, trying to stuff one of her arms into a sleeve. She was shaking so badly that she could barely speak. "Gonna need the blanket to make a tent."

"No," Jackie said. "You put it on."

Sidney shook her head and so did Jackie.

They were both stubborn. Each thought the other needed the jacket most. And then they realized, without saying so, that they were too tired, cold, and wet to argue. They needed to rest before either of them could do anything more. Wrapping both the blanket and the jacket around themselves they huddled silently together and accepted what little warmth there was between them. The rocks overhead provided some relief from the rain, and after a few minutes, Sidney felt she was ready to carry on.

The first thing she did was to find the painkillers in her pack. She gave two to Jackie, along with a sip of water from the water bottle to wash them down. She insisted that Jackie keep the jacket on.

"I'll warm up once I start moving around," she said.

Then she went to work on fashioning what shelter she

could for herself and Jackie. The activity loosened up her fingers and allowed her at last to untie the knot from around her waist. The segment of rope was long enough to serve as one lashing and the three metres of rope she'd cut earlier provided the three other pieces she needed.

Instructing Jackie to shine the flashlight under the trees, Sidney found four spruce cones, which she then wrapped in the corners of the blanket. She secured the segments of rope around them with clove hitch knots, and then tied two of the blanket's corners to large, deeply buried rocks in the outcropping. The other two corners she fastened to the two strongest looking trees in the grove.

The relief from the rain was immediate.

Sidney then turned to the task of making a fire. She snapped and cut off dry boughs and dead branches that had been sheltered from the rain on the undersides of the trees and piled up twigs, spruce cones, and old man's beard to use for kindling.

She thought she was working too slowly – it felt like hours were passing. But to Jackie, what Sidney was doing seemed miraculously fast. She was holding the beam of light wherever Sidney's hands were working and those hands still looked like chubby baby hands to Jackie. How had her baby sister learned to do all this? The more Jackie watched those little fingers working, the worse she felt. It was her fault they were in this situation. She couldn't sit doing nothing while

Sidney struggled alone to save their lives.

Jackie pressed her back against the mountain and, shifting her weight onto her good leg and supporting herself with her hands, began to inch her way up along the rock wall.

Sidney had been talking to Jackie all the while as she constructed the shelter and gathered fire materials – she knew it was important to make sure Jackie remained alert – so she'd been babbling about everything and nothing, through chattering teeth.

At the moment Jackie was trying to stand, she was saying, "Too bad I can't make a real lean-to, hey Jackie? 'Member that lean-to we built in Forest Wardens when we went winter camping?" She had forgotten that Jackie had not gone on that camping trip. She heard a noise and turned around. Jackie was on her feet, clutching at the rocks behind her to support herself, and hunched over to avoid hitting her head on the canopy Sidney had erected. She took a little hopping step forward.

"What are you doing?!" Sidney shouted.

"I want to help...." Jackie said, and took another step. Her good leg felt like it was made of rubber. She began to tremble.

"No! Sit down!" Sidney scrambled to her feet and took a step toward Jackie, just as Jackie's good leg crumpled and her sore ankle touched down. Jackie gasped, collapsing.

"What are you doing?!" Sidney shrieked again. She stood,

*looking down at Jackie in horror as she clutched at her foot,
rolling back and forth and crying from pain.*

SIDNEY, JACKIE, AND CHRIS had been dropped off at their
school by their parents at 7:30 in the morning, and the
bus destined for Camp Snowberry was rolling by 7:45.

The first hour on the bus was uneventful.

Sidney shared a seat with Kate, who was making up a
long story about her rings and their various powers and
the adventures one might have while wearing them. The
problem was, Kate's story wasn't very well developed, and
she kept going back to change things.

"The ruby ring is the Ring of Time. Anyone who
wears it can stop time or make time go faster, see?"

Sidney nodded.

"So one day this girl named Lukamonga, which means
'wolf-child' in her world, was wearing it and she saw a
little, baby, injured wolf crying for its mother. So she
said...." Kate stopped talking, then started again. "No, wait
a minute. The ruby ring isn't the Ring of Time, it's the Ring
of Animal Voices. The sapphire ring is the Ring of Time.
So Lukamonga was wearing the ruby ring, but it wasn't the
Ring of Time, it was the Ring of Animal Voices, so she was
able to understand what the baby wolf was saying...."

Kate went on in this way. Sidney began to grow very

confused about which ring held which power, and soon the sun shining in through the window, and the motion of the bus, and the sound of Kate's voice droning on caused Sidney's head to droop and wobble from side to side. It finally found a resting place on Kate's shoulder.

While Sidney dozed and mumbled the occasional "uh huh" at the appropriate places in Kate's story, Jackie sat at the back of the bus with the rest of the Grade Six class and tried to work out for herself how she was going to get through the next few days. Courtney was ignoring her. She wasn't being mean, she was just pretending Jackie didn't exist. So far, Erica and the other girls in Courtney's group hadn't noticed that Courtney was ignoring Jackie, which was good. As soon as they noticed, Jackie was fully aware, they would start to ignore her too.

As she pondered her situation and racked her brains to think of ways to head off the inevitable misery of her fate at Camp Snowberry, she heard Carter call her name.

"Jackie. Jackie!"

She turned her head to see that Carter was holding something in his hand.

"Look at this."

He was holding a tiny garter snake.

"Ahhh," Jackie cooed. "He's so cute. Where'd you get him?"

"Caught him in the ravine."

"Whoa! You must be fast. Those things move so quick."

Carter looked very pleased with himself. "We're going to put him in Mrs. Waldren's sleeping bag tonight."

Jackie felt dismay at the thought of the poor little snake suffocating in the bottom of a sleeping bag, but she was careful not to let it show on her face.

"Don't you think that might be scary?"

"That's the whole point."

"No, I mean for the snake."

Jackie felt eyes on her and glanced up to see that Courtney was suddenly very much aware of her existence on planet earth.

"Let me see," Courtney demanded.

Carter dangled the snake near Courtney's head. It stretched and darted toward her face. Courtney squealed, drawing the attention of Mr. Kingsley, who was several rows ahead of them, sharing a seat with Chris.

"What's going on back there?" he asked.

"Nothing," several voices chorused.

"Keep quiet!" Carter angrily hissed at Courtney. He turned away from her and back to Jackie.

"You think it would scare him?" he asked.

"Well, he might die. He might get squished, or maybe not be able to breathe."

Carter nodded.

"It would've been funny though. To freak out Waldren," Jackie heard herself saying.

She didn't usually talk that way. She never referred to teachers by their last names. But a thought was forming in Jackie's mind. Maybe there were less risky ways to take power away from Courtney Strachan-Smith than doing what Chris had done. Courtney lived for attention from boys; she considered herself the queen, but in her world, Carter Leavitt was certainly the king. It seemed to Jackie that Carter liked her, at least for the moment, more than he liked Courtney. It seemed there might be a way to make that work.

"Hey, Jackie," Courtney called.

Jackie looked at her.

"Where'd you get those shorts?"

Jackie tensed for a moment before answering, trying to prepare a response to the put-down she was sure was coming.

"The mall."

"Oh. They look really good on you."

For the first time all year, Jackie gave Courtney a dismissive look.

"Thanks," she coolly replied.

It was working already.

And maybe it would have kept working, but Jackie never got the chance to find out. Too many things went wrong.

CHAPTER 19

"I WANTED TO HELP," JACKIE SOBBED THROUGH HER TEARS. *"You're not helping, you're being stupid!" Sidney was kneeling next to Jackie, holding the flashlight's beam on her ankle and examining it closely. It was still the ugliest, purplest, most twisted ankle she'd ever seen, but it looked no worse than before.*

She felt her anger return. She reached for her backpack and rifled through it for the painkillers. Frustrated at not being able to find them quickly, she dumped the contents out. She found the pills, opened the container and shook two more onto her hand, which, along with the water bottle, she thrust at Jackie.

"Take these."

"Stop shouting at me!" Jackie cried. "Stop bossing me around!"

"You're being stupid!"

"I'm not stupid!"

A great gust of wind caught the blanket and it flapped noisily and strained against the knots Sidney had made.

The sky lit up over their heads, illuminating the fear on each of their faces for the other to see. They braced themselves for the crack of thunder they knew was coming, but it was much louder than what they could prepare for.

Boom! Boom!

Jackie and Sidney were both crying now.

The thunder bounced from mountaintop to mountaintop, echoing around them and finally dying down until, once more, the only sound they heard was the relentless rain.

They were cold, and wet. Jackie was in pain and Sidney was exhausted. The sky rained on. Dark closed in all around them, not afternoon-storm dark, not dusk dark, but real nighttime-in-the-mountains-without-the-stars dark.

THE BUS BROKE DOWN thirty kilometres from Camp Snowberry. As the wait for a replacement dragged on, the campers grew hot and restless. Mr. Kingsley, Mrs. Waldren, and Mrs. Talmadge had no choice but to allow the students to get off the stuffy vehicle. Everyone was told to stay nearby, and they did, mostly, except for Carter and William Beach, who snuck off to share a cigarette while the teachers were preoccupied with Kate, whose asthma had flared up. Her puffers didn't seem to be helping.

When the two boys returned, Mr. Kingsley was immediately suspicious.

"I smell smoke," he said. "Every one of you knows the rules. You'll all be better off if someone tells me who, right now."

No one spoke.

"All right then, line up right here."

Mr. Kingsley went down the line, pausing to take a breath next to each of the students. When he was four people away from Carter Leavitt, Jackie spoke up.

"Mr. Kingsley?"

"Yes?" Jackie was one of his favourite students.

"What if your parents smoke?"

"I know your parents don't smoke, Jackie."

"But some parents do. And the smell stays on people's clothes, even on their kids' clothes. So it's not really fair to send someone home unless you actually catch them smoking, right?"

"Well, I don't think...." Mr. Kingsley didn't get a chance to finish, as Kate started coughing again.

The three teacher-chaperones took Kate back onto the bus and the students dismissed themselves from the smoke-sniffing lineup. Carter walked over to Jackie.

"Thanks," he whispered. "I was sweatin'. How'd ya think of that?"

Jackie shrugged, as if to say, "I spend all my time thinking my way out of trouble."

She pointed at Carter's backpack. "You better get rid of those smokes though."

Carter pursed his lips and nodded. "Wonder what I should do with them."

Sidney came over to where they were standing.

"Jackie?"

Jackie seemed not to hear her. Sidney tapped her arm.

"Jackie?"

"What?!"

The way Jackie said "what" was different from the way she'd ever said it before. Sometimes when Sidney called to her sister or tapped her on the arm, Jackie replied "what" in a way that implied distraction or boredom or even mild impatience. But for the most part, when Sidney called, Jackie gladly came. Hearing Jackie say, "What?!" in a way that meant "I don't want you around me," hurt Sidney.

"You don't hafta bite my head off," she said.

"What do you want?"

"You think Kate's okay?"

"Yeah, she's fine."

"Could you come on the bus with me to check on her?"

"I will later. She's fine."

Sidney stared at her sister, mystified, then walked away. She went off to find Chris, who was leaning against a tree, reading a book.

"Chris, will you go on the bus with me to check on Kate? Jackie won't."

Chris glanced in Jackie's direction. She was with Carter.

"Yeah, come on," Chris said to Sidney. They boarded the broken-down bus together.

CHAPTER 20

"I'M SORRY," JACKIE SAID, PRESSING HER FISTS AGAINST *her eyes to try to stop the tears.*

Sidney made no attempt to stop crying. She was tossing things back into her backpack. "Why wouldn't you come on the bus to check on Katie? I don't even know if she's okay!"

"I'm sorry," Jackie repeated.

"Why do you hafta be friends with Courtney and that...that," she spat it out, *"idiot! Carter Leavitt. Why can't you forgive Chris for whatever it is he did, and...."*

Jackie interrupted, surprised. "Chris didn't do anything."

"But he never sits with you anymore. He won't even come over when Mom makes you call him."

"That's because...." Jackie searched for words to try to explain the disintegration of her friendship with Chris. But she hadn't yet been able to understand it herself. She knew it

was her fault, she just didn't know how to explain it. Her words trailed away. "He didn't do anything."

Sidney didn't seem to be listening anymore. She was looking around frantically, shining the light everywhere.

"Where are my matches?"

She emptied the backpack again and pawed through the contents – her duct tape, her log book and pencil, her candle, her whistle, her first aid kit, her fishing line, a sweatshirt ("Here, put this on," she said, tossing it Jackie's way), her spare batteries, her compass, her food pack, her water bottle, her small pot...no waterproof match container.

She stood up and looked where she had been crouched. They weren't there. She and Jackie patted the ground beneath Jackie's spot. Nothing but a couple of pebbles.

Sidney passed the light slowly, centimetre by centimetre, back and forth across the ledge.

"There!" Jackie said, pointing.

A puff of wind sent something tumbling across the edge of the beam. Sidney cast her light where Jackie was pointing, just in time to see another gust catch the matches and send them sliding off the ledge.

Sidney flattened herself on her belly and scuttled across the floor of the ledge like a lizard. She held the flashlight in her right hand and peered over the ledge. The matches were resting precariously against a mossy rock. No longer protected by the blanket, she was drenched once more as she stretched out her hand. Her arm was too short. She inched forward.

"Be careful!" Jackie said. She had remained where she was, under the canopy, and could see nothing but Sidney's feet. "What's happening? Do you see them?"

Sidney could hear Jackie's questions. She was so close.

"I've almost got them!"

She pushed herself a little farther.

A sudden blast from the wind lifted the matches. Desperately, Sidney lunged.

She lost her grip on the flashlight, and they both went tumbling over the ledge.

Her scream ripped through the wind and the rain, piercing Jackie's eardrums.

THE REPLACEMENT BUS DRIVER WAS BLACK. Sidney and Jackie had seen dark-skinned Black people before. There were many Africans in the congregation of Papa's church. Papa was dark brown. But neither Jackie nor Sidney, and certainly no one else who boarded the bus and filed past the new driver, had ever seen a person that was truly Black like this man.

Everyone, even the teachers, noticed his deep, ebony colour. But none of them, not the teachers or the students, were the kind of people to react or comment on a person's colour. Except for William.

He stared at the driver for a moment. Then, "Whoa," he said.

"Pardon me?" the driver asked. He had a heavy accent.

"Nothin'." William giggled and poked Carter, who had boarded ahead of him and just behind Jackie. Carter giggled as well. The two of them shuffled to their places near the back of the bus and collapsed, still giggling, into their seats. Even Courtney and Erica cast them disapproving glances.

Discomfort began to settle over Jackie. She was confused, and uncertain of what had just happened. Were they making fun of the driver? Were they making fun of him because he was ebony Black?

She sat quietly, thinking, her stomach in knots. Should she confront them? Should she ask what they thought they were doing? But what if she had misunderstood? Maybe William wasn't even talking about the driver when he said "whoa." Maybe one of the boys on the bus had belched. It wasn't like it never happened. Maybe that's what he was referring to, and the cause of his laughing fit.

She looked over at Chris and wished she could ask him what he thought. But she couldn't.

Then something occurred to her. William and Carter knew her mother was Black, right? They knew Sidney was her sister, and Sidney looked more Black than she did. "They know I'm Black, and they like me," she thought to herself. "So I must be wrong. They wouldn't make fun of a Black man in front of me. I'm their friend. They like me. They like me."

She turned around to look at Carter. He winked at her. Her heart did a little flip-flop. He liked her. She settled back into her seat and the knot in her stomach went away. Almost.

CAMP SNOWBERRY was named by its owner, Carol Cardinal, for the small white berries that grew everywhere on the slopes of the property. Here she had built a camp to which she invited school and church groups, social agencies, and health centres to bring children and teach them about nature. The campgrounds were in a heavily forested area, and Mrs. Cardinal had taken great care to clear away as few trees as possible in the building of the cabins, the cookhouse, and the firepit. The silver stream that ran through the land was clear and pure, and hiking trails spread out from the firepit like threads from a spider's web.

Neither Sidney nor Jackie had been to Camp Snowberry, but they had been nearby. The provincial campground where they had tented with their parents on numerous occasions was not far away. Sidney recognized the landscape. She wanted to shout to Jackie that Brid's tree was just over the hill, past those cliffs and up the path toward Becker's Pass, but she was still angry with her, so she said nothing.

The students, with the exception of Kate, were given their cabin assignments and instructed to unpack their clothing and meet at the firepit with their backpacks in fifteen minutes. Kate, by now audibly wheezing, was rushed into Mrs. Cardinal's ranch house by the worried teachers.

Sidney hurriedly emptied her bags, then raced off toward the ranch house. She met Mr. Kingsley, wearing a frown, coming down the path toward her.

"Is Kate okay?" she asked him.

He shook his head. "We're calling her parents. I'm afraid she's too sick to stay."

"Oh no!" Sidney wailed. All the fun she and Kate had planned for their time at Camp Snowberry flew away on dragonfly wings into the beautiful blue sky. "Can I go see her?"

"You should meet with the other campers now, Sidney."

"Please? Is she crying?"

"She is crying, yes." He sighed and rubbed his forehead. Never in all his years of taking students to Camp Snowberry had a trip started this badly. "She might feel better if you're with her. Go on then."

Sidney ran toward the house.

When Mr. Kingsley reached the firepit, the campers

were waiting for him there, with the exception of two.

"Where are William and Carter?" he demanded.

Before anyone had a chance to answer, the two boys came dashing from the bushes behind the cookhouse. The smell of cigarettes trailed after them like ribbons from a kite.

"Sit down!" Mr. Kingsley barked. He was tired, he was worried about his asthmatic student, and he was in no mood for nonsense. He took both their backpacks, opened them, and shook the contents into the dirt. Many items tumbled out – pens, notebooks, drawing pads, water bottles – all the things they were supposed to have.

"Who's holding the cigarettes?" he asked the circle of students, who were silently watching him. No one answered.

"Do I·have to make every one of you empty those bags?"

Except for the birds in the trees calling out to one another, there was not a sound.

Mr. Kingsley pointed to the student sitting nearest him, who happened to be Elizabeth Kinnie. She took each article out of her bag and placed it neatly on the ground in front of her. He pointed to the next student, Dallas, who did the same, and beside her, Starr, who did the same. Jackie was next.

Her hands shook as she slowly unzipped her backpack. She had never been in trouble. In all her years in school, she had never seen the inside of the principal's office.

She reached in, pulled out the cigarette package, and held it in her hand. She didn't look at Mr. Kingsley.

"Are those yours, Jackie?"

She heard the shock and disappointment in his voice and couldn't bring herself to answer. She let her hair hang to cover her face, which was burning.

"I think your parents will be very sad to hear from me. Do you want to tell me whose cigarettes those are before I make the call?"

Probably in the entire history of kids sitting around a firepit, there has never been this much silence, Jackie thought. It couldn't have been more quiet if there had been no one there at all. Even the birds had stopped singing.

Someone spoke up. "They're not hers. She.... She. I don't think she knew they were there."

It was Chris.

"Do you know who they belong to, Chris?" Mr. Kingsley asked.

Chris nodded.

"Who?"

Chris looked at Jackie. She felt his eyes on her and

looked up, and they stared at each other for what seemed like a long time. She could see a hundred different emotions in his eyes.

This would be the time, Jackie thought, for Carter to speak up. Please, please, Carter....

But Carter said nothing.

"Chris?" Mr. Kingsley was still waiting.

Chris answered quietly, "They're mine."

Mr. Kingsley laughed. It was a sour, tired little laugh. More like a bark or a cough.

"I see. Well, let's have you smoke one. Let's see if you know how. Jackie, give those cigarettes to Chris."

Jackie didn't move.

Mr. Kingsley stomped over to her, snatched the package from her hand, and tossed it to Chris. It landed at his feet.

"Go ahead."

"They're not his," Jackie said.

"Whose are they?"

Jackie didn't know what to say. She knew Mr. Kingsley wouldn't believe her if she claimed they were hers. She knew he didn't believe they belonged to Chris either. She couldn't bring herself to tell the truth.

"Go on, Chris," Mr. Kingsley said.

Chris slowly bent over and picked up the cigarettes. He held them awkwardly, turned them over in his hand, studying the box, trying to see how to open it. When he'd figured it out, he withdrew one of its contents and cautiously raised it to his lips.

"That's the wrong end."

Chris took the cigarette out of his mouth.

"I know," he said. "You're making me nervous."

He turned it around and sat there.

Jackie couldn't tell who looked more miserable, Mr. Kingsley or Chris.

"Where's your lighter? Where're your matches? Come on Chris – smokers keep something to light up with. Go on."

Chris had no matches and no lighter. Nevertheless, he pretended to search his pockets. He opened his mouth to say, "I can't find them," and the cigarette fell from his lips. He fumbled clumsily to catch it, but it bounced off his knee and into the dirt.

Just at that moment, Mrs. Waldren came racing toward them, Sidney at her heels.

"Richard," she said to Mr. Kingsley, "I think we're going to have to get an ambulance from Canmore. She'll be blue by the time her parents get here."

"Okay. Make the call. Go! I'm right behind you!"

Mrs. Waldren and Sidney ran back toward the house.

"Don't move!" Mr. Kingsley looked around the circle of students fiercely. "Not one of you. I'll send Mrs.

Talmadge back here to wait with you. We have a serious emergency to deal with now, and you're all old enough to act responsibly. Don't move!"

He hurried away.

The silence continued. Jackie thought about the puzzlement and hurt on the bus driver's face when Carter and William were laughing at him.

A few students scuffed their feet in the dirt. William Beach was the first to speak. He muttered to Carter, "What an idiot. Didn't even know which end was the filter."

Although he was muttering, everyone heard.

Carter picked up two little sticks and threw them in Chris's direction. "I thought you junior forest boys could start a fire with twigs."

One of the twigs hit Chris on the cheek. He stood up, walked over to Carter, and punched him as hard as he could in the face. The circle of students erupted.

Carter and Chris rolled around in the dirt, throwing punches. Some of the younger children were crying. Starr and Lindsay ran toward the ranch house screaming for Mr. Kingsley.

Carter had been in many fights. He was more experienced at this sort of thing than Chris, but Chris had rage on his side. He was managing well enough until Jackie threw herself in between them.

"Stop it, stop it, stop it!" she cried. She was on her

knees in the dirt, trying to separate them. "Chris, don't!" She managed to get hold of one of his arms and pulled on it. This momentary distraction was just the opening Carter needed. His foot shot out and he caught Chris directly in the face with his foot. Everyone heard the Crack! as Chris's nose broke. Blood spurted out.

Several people screamed.

Chris staggered blindly to his feet, holding his nose. Blood poured through his fingers.

Jackie shrieked at Carter, who was still lying on the ground. "You coward! Stupid, stupid coward!"

She ran to Chris, who was stumbling up the path. He shook her hand from his arm.

"Leave me alone," he coughed.

"Let me help you."

"I mean it!"

Jackie stood and watched as Chris, blinded by pain, staggered off in the wrong direction. Dallas and Elizabeth came up behind him, each taking an arm, and guided him toward the house.

Jackie turned and ran. It was an hour before anyone noticed she was missing.

CHAPTER 21

For about five seconds, Jackie was paralyzed *with fear.*

"Sidney?" she called. "Sidney!"

She crawled on her hands and knees across the ledge, in the direction she thought Sidney had gone. The darkness was total. She flattened herself on her belly and slid forward slowly, just as Sidney had done, feeling for the end of the ledge with her hands. When her hands felt nothing, she stopped.

Her ankle screamed and the blood pounded in her head.

"Sidney!!"

A small voice sounded, nearer than she had expected.

"Jackie?"

Jackie's heart leapt. Her sister was alive!

"Where are you?" she asked.

"I'm, I'm holding onto a bush."

"Do you have the flashlight? Can you see my hand?" Jackie waved her hand back and forth.

"I dropped it."

"Okay." Jackie stopped to think. "We could use some lightning right now, hey, Sister?"

"Yes."

"I'm going to reach down. See if I can touch you, all right?"

"My arms are hurting, Jackie. I can't hold on much longer."

Jackie tried to keep her voice calm.

"I'll get you." She reached over the ledge and cautiously swept her arm around. Nothing.

Then it came — the most welcome bolt of lightning.

Sidney saw Jackie, Jackie saw Sidney.

Sidney had fallen too far out of Jackie's reach.

CONFUSION AND CHAOS reigned at Camp Snowberry in the moments after Chris's nose was broken. When Elizabeth and Dallas led Chris into the ranch house, Sidney was as horrified as everyone else to see his bleeding, swollen face. She tried to find out what had happened, but it was a bit like being a shrill little bee buzzing around in the ears of those present. No one had time to think about Sidney – Kate and Chris were the priorities. She gathered that Chris's accident had something to do with Jackie, and in the turmoil of her mind, she assumed that Jackie had been hurt as well.

She bolted from the house in search of her sister, a search that led her in and out of every cabin on the premises, without success. None of the Grade Sixes seemed to know where Jackie had gone, and none of them cared at that particular moment. They were all watching as the air ambulance hovered overhead, preparing to land. Most of the camp staff were occupied with trying to keep the students back so that the helicopter could touch down.

After twenty minutes of futile seeking, Sidney's concern grew to sickening fear. It occurred to her that Jackie might have done a very, very foolish thing by running off into the bush without proper gear, dressed in a pair of shorts and a tank top.

Sidney tried to do everything exactly right after that. She finally found a camp staffer who would listen to her, and together they went to Mr. Kingsley, who was with the air ambulance attendants, who were ministering to both Kate and Chris.

"We're going to have to get them both to Calgary ASAP," the female attendant was saying to Mr. Kingsley when Sidney and the counsellor burst in with their news that Jackie was missing.

Mr. Kingsley stared at them blankly for a moment as he tried to force his reeling mind to focus on what they were saying.

"How long has she been gone?" he asked.

"No one seems to know."

Mr. Kingsley shook his head, disbelieving. "There's no end to the trouble some days will bring," he said heavily.

"All right." He turned back to the helicopter medic. "I'm not going with you. We have a missing student here. Delores!" he called to Mrs. Talmadge, who left Chris's side and hurried over. "I'm going to have to send you with these two on the chopper. Jackie Bailey has gone missing."

"Oh, dear Lord," Mrs. Talmadge sighed. "Right, I'll get my things."

Mr. Kingsley sent Sidney out with the counsellor, whose name was Robin, with strict instructions to gather all the students in the cookhouse and allow no one to leave the campgrounds for any reason whatsoever.

"I've got to call the RCMP and your parents, Sidney. Help Robin with the head count. There should be forty-two of you, minus Kate, Chris, and Jackie." He seemed to realize, at the last moment, that his tone was sharp, and how worried Sidney was. He placed a hand on top of her head and patted it.

"I'm sure she's close by. Probably just went off to think. We'll find her."

Sidney nodded, and she and Robin left the house.

They were silent as they walked down the path together toward the cabins. In that time, a terrible argument took place in Sidney's mind.

Everything she had been taught in Junior Forest Wardens told her she should obey Mr. Kingsley. She knew there were good reasons why he didn't want anyone leaving the grounds. She liked Mr. Kingsley and didn't want to add to his troubles. She knew he was probably right about Jackie having gone off to think.

But she also knew other things. She knew it would take precious time to organize a proper search, maybe as much as a half-hour or even an hour. What if Jackie had been hurt in the fight that broke Chris's nose? Every minute spent organizing could put her at risk. She knew they would probably not allow her to go along with them on the search, even if she told them she thought Jackie had gone to Brid's tree. They would ask her for directions and go off without her, and Brid's tree was hard to find. What if they missed it? Uppermost in her mind was the image of Jackie, limping along the path, maybe bleeding, angry over whatever had happened to Chris, maybe crying. Alone and afraid. Sidney couldn't bear it. She made up her mind. She would find Jackie and bring her back.

"I'll see if anyone's in those cabins," she said, pointing

to the group of three that included the one where her gear was stored.

Robin nodded and hurried off in the direction of cabins four, five, and six.

Luckily, Sidney found cabin two was empty. The first thing she did was write a note, drawing a map explaining as best she could where she had gone. She dug to the bottom of her backpack for her log book and pencil, hastily scribbled the note, and placed it, addressed to Mr. Kingsley, on top of the chest of drawers.

She gathered up her backpack, heart pounding. As a second thought, just before leaving, she went back to her suitcase and pulled out her raincoat. It was sunny now, but Sidney knew how quickly weather could change in the mountains. She slipped out the door and scuttled silently around the side of the building that could not be seen from the cookhouse. Glancing guiltily over her shoulder all the while, she headed for the bushes behind the cabins and ducked down low to crawl through them. She came out on a path that she was certain would take her in the direction of Becker's Pass.

She was off.

She didn't see, as the door latched behind her, the note she had written, caught by the draft created by the door's closing, lift up and sail across the room, to the floor and underneath a bunk bed.

CHAPTER 22

JACKIE SLIPPED OUT OF THE RAINCOAT AND WRAPPED
the end of one sleeve tightly around her wrist. The sweatshirt, which she had managed to keep dry until now, was
immediately drenched and she felt icy cold again.

"I'm slipping," Sidney said. Her arms were shaking.

Jackie slid over to the left, until she thought she was
above the place where she'd seen Sidney. She clenched her
teeth hard, forcing the pain in her foot from her mind.

"Grab the raincoat," she said. "I'll pull you up."

She lowered the raincoat slowly. Sidney could hear it
coming, and then at last she felt it brush her face.

"It's here, I've got it, Jackie!"

Sidney loosened one trembling hand from the branch it
was holding and clutched at the dangling sleeve of the rain-

coat. It was wet. She did what Jackie had done, winding the end of the sleeve around her wrist to gain a better grip. Then she felt around beneath her with one of her feet, until she found a tiny crook in which to plant the toe of her boot.

"I'm ready," she said.

Jackie did as Sidney had done, scuffling behind herself with her good leg. She found a well-anchored rock and hooked her foot around it.

"So am I. One, two, three...."

Jackie pulled.

Using her free hand to clutch at bits of scrubby bushes and her feet to anchor where she could, Sidney progressed little by little. Jackie strained to hold on as she listened to Sidney's efforts.

Finally, Sidney's free hand felt the safe flatness of the ledge. She felt around for something to grab.

"Ow!" Jackie winced.

"Sorry," Sidney said. She let go of Jackie's hair.

Jackie clutched Sidney's collar and helped her scramble onto the ledge. The two of them crawled beneath the shelter of the blanket and lay there, soaked to the skin, panting, but safe together again.

FOR A LONG TIME, *the girls were too drained to do anything except lie on the floor of their shelter together under the raincoat.*

"The rain is slowing down," Sidney finally said.

"Do you think they'll come looking for us tonight if it stops?" Jackie's voice was hoarse.

"No," Sidney replied. "Too dangerous."

"What if they don't find us tomorrow?" Jackie asked. "What if we're lost here for good?"

"We're not lost," Sidney answered.

"What do you mean?"

"I know where Brid's tree is, and I know how to get back to Camp Snowberry from Brid's tree. I'll go back there in the morning and bring them to you."

Jackie allowed Sidney's words to sink in.

They weren't lost.

They worked together to make themselves as comfortable as possible. Jackie took the last of the painkillers, and between the two of them, they drained the water bottle. Sidney set her cooking pot out to catch a rivulet of water pouring off a corner of the blanket. The rain was definitely slowing down and they didn't want to be left with none. They hungrily ate the cereal bar and more of the trail mix from Sidney's food pack.

The spruce boughs Sidney had gathered earlier were of no use for a fire, now that the matches had gone over the mountain.

She flung one against the rocks. "I'm so clumsy!"

"You are not."

"*I lost the flashlight* and *the matches! You know how cold it gets in the mountains overnight!*"

Jackie had to admit to herself that a fire would have been welcome. She recalled many mountain camping trips when she had thought she would freeze to death — and those sleeps had all taken place in dry clothes wrapped in a sleeping bag. Here she was, wet, cold, hungry, her ankle throbbing — but she couldn't help feeling more alive, and happier about it, than she'd ever felt before.

"*It doesn't matter.*" *She began to gather Sidney's spruce boughs around them.* "*We can use these for a bed.*"

Sidney helped spread them *across the floor, but they were so dry and prickly that the girls decided the earth beneath them was best. They lay down again and covered themselves in the raincoat.*

"*It's just like in our game,*" *Jackie muttered.* "*Only you're the big sister who knows how to do everything and I'm the baby.*"

"*Say we open our eyes and we're back at home,*" *Sidney said.*

"*Yeah,*" *Jackie replied.* "*And say we never play this game again.*"

They both laughed a little.

There was nothing more they could do but wait for

morning. They were cramped and uncomfortable, but that couldn't be helped. Jackie was exhausted.

"Sidney?" she said groggily. "You know how you said you love me more than everything that has a name?"

"Yeah."

"Well, I love you even more than that."

Sidney was quiet for a long time. Then she said, "I felt like I was saying goodbye to you."

"When?"

"Every day. For the last year."

It was Jackie's turn to be silent. "I'm sorry," she said at last.

"Will my friends turn into people like Courtney and Erica in Grade Six? Will Chris turn into Carter?"

Jackie snorted. "Chris will always be Chris. Carter's nothing but a...."

Jackie suddenly sat bolt upright.

"What is it?" Sidney hissed. "Do you hear a bear?"

"Carter's matches! They're still in my pocket."

BY NOW THE RAIN had slowed to a drizzle. Sidney gathered more boughs and, by the light of the moon and a few stars that had showed themselves, replenished her supply of twigs, sticks, spruce cones and needles, and the driest bits of old man's beard. She cut a few lengths of fishing line and used *them to bind the sticks together to form fire bundles. Then she carefully laid everything out in the way she had been taught.*

Most of the matches were damp. Jackie held her breath as Sidney struck one, then another, then another, with no spark.

"How many are left?" Jackie asked.

"Four."

Very carefully, Sidney tried to strike another match, but the head crumbled. The next one sparked briefly, then immediately died out. With shaking hands, she struck again. This time the match caught and Sidney held it to the old man's beard. The flame licked the lichen, then ran along the dry spruce cones and needles and ignited those. Very gently, she blew on the flame as it spread to the twigs. It took! Sidney's fire grew from the twigs to the sticks and from the sticks to the branches.

She poured some of the rainwater she had caught into her water bottle, then boiled the rest to make a thin soup from the bouillon cubes she carried in her food pack. They shared the last of the trail mix and a fruit leather, and washed it all down with sips of water.

It was the most delicious meal either of them had ever eaten, they agreed.

Sidney piled more of her bundles on the fire and stirred it up with a stick. Close to the flames, she could see that her

Forest Wardens shirt was filthy and wrinkled.

"This'll never come clean," she said.

There was no reply from Jackie. Sidney glanced over, and saw by the light of the dancing orange blaze that she was asleep.

For a long time, Sidney crouched next to the fire, watching as the sky cleared and constellations that she recognized appeared. Gala had been named after a constellation watcher – Galileo.

Sidney felt a slight twinge of hurt when she thought of Gala; a sense that he had let her down. She had needed help a thousand times in the hours that had just passed. She had needed strong magic, but it hadn't come.

Maybe her mother was right. Maybe magic wasn't real.

She placed another bundle on the fire, then crept over to where Jackie slept and crawled in next to her.

CHAPTER 23

SIDNEY OPENED HER EYES. SHE WAS SO STIFF THAT IT *hurt to move and her right arm was numb. No wonder – Jackie's head was lying on it like a stone. She was damp and icy cold. Her breath formed little white clouds over her head.*

She carefully wriggled her arm from beneath Jackie's head and unfolded her creaking body. Then she heard the whir of helicopter propellers in the distance.

They were coming closer! A jolt of energy surged through her. She snatched up the tank top Jackie had removed the night before and scrambled to her feet, stumbling unsteadily toward the sound, which was coming from above the ridge. Ignoring the jelly in her legs, Sidney made herself climb – huffing and blowing, half crawling, half running up the mountain, toward the path and Brid's tree. But there was too much ground to cover, and it was still wet and slippery. She couldn't get to the open space on the path.

She braced herself and waved the shirt, shouting at the top of her lungs, "Here, here, here!"

Had they spotted her? The helicopter pilot circled back and then circled around again until he was nearly directly over Sidney's head. Yes, he knew she was there! He waved to her, then circled east and rapidly zoomed off. There was nowhere to land safely, Sidney knew that. But help was on the way.

Sidney became aware that her body was trembling. She sank weakly and allowed herself to melt against the mountain. Help was coming and they would be all right. She lay flat against the earth and rocks and scrubby grass and drank in the smell of their morning-chilled freshness.

Her eyes focused on two little blossoms sprouting from a sheltered place beneath a rock.

Fairy bells.

She didn't care what anyone thought. It didn't matter to her if no one else believed.

"Life is magic," she said.

CHAPTER 24

JACKIE WOKE FROM HER SURGERY AND LAY FOR SEVERAL minutes with her eyes closed, listening to the sounds around her. It wasn't that she didn't want anyone to know she was awake. She wasn't trying to eavesdrop; she just couldn't open her eyes at first. It was as though she was floating slowly through an ocean of air, rising up from a deep place, breaking through an invisible screen.

The first thing she knew was that she was warm. The second thing she knew was that her family was with her. She heard the murmuring of voices that belonged to her mother and father, her grandparents. She heard Papa's deep rumble humming a song. When she was finally able to open her eyes, she saw a little glass vase on the table next to her bed. Brid's tail feather was sticking out of it. Through bleary eyes, she saw her parents standing at the window with their arms around one another; Grandma and Grandpa Bailey sitting on the bed across from hers; Nana crocheting in an armchair. And she saw Sidney. She was sitting in Papa's lap, head against his chest, as he rocked her.

Sidney was the first to notice Jackie was awake. She flew out of Papa's arms to Jackie's side, shouting, "Hey!" And then the others all gathered around, and Earl put out a hand to restrain Sidney from jumping on the bed.

"Careful. Remember her ankle," he warned.

"Does it hurt?" Mary asked, looking anxiously into Jackie's face.

Jackie nodded. "A little." Her mouth felt like it was stuffed with moss.

Her mother helped her sit up, her father let Sidney crank up the bed to support Jackie's back, and Grandpa hurried off to get the nurse, who said, "Well, hello, Miss Jackie," when she came into the room.

Jackie feebly waved in reply.

"Did your mom and dad tell you what we did?"

Jackie shook her head no.

Her limbs felt heavy and useless. Her eyes rolled as she attempted to get them to rest on the nurse's face as she bustled around, fiddling with the tubes that were dripping fluid into Jackie's arm. Finally, Jackie was able to see the nurse's name tag – "Betty Ann Lamoureux, R.N.," it said.

"Dr. Lane reset your broken ankle. He had to insert a

couple of pins. You'll be on crutches for a while, but you won't have a limp or anything when it heals. You'll be good as new. Except for a scar. You were a little dehydrated, a little hypothermic, and we're taking care of that. All in all, things could have been much worse."

Jackie looked at Sidney. "I could have died if you hadn't come," the look said. She didn't have to say it out loud. They both knew.

Betty Ann Lamoureux sent everyone out. She insisted that they go to the cafeteria for lunch.

"I've never seen such a stubborn group of people," she said to Jackie after they'd left. "Do you think I could get them out of here? Your parents left for five minutes this afternoon to see Chris, and your sister went to see her little friend down in respiratory and was back before I blinked."

Jackie's stomach gave a little jump. Chris was there.

"Let's have a look at this foot," Betty Ann said, and as she gently pulled back the blankets that covered Jackie's ankle, Jackie summoned up the nerve to ask her question.

"Uhhmm," she started.

"Yes?"

"Is his nose broken?" Her voice sounded strange to her own ears – groggy and low.

"Oh, yes," the nurse replied. "Badly." She shook her head. "I don't understand what goes on with kids these days."

"It wasn't Chris's fault," Jackie said.

"That right?"

Jackie nodded.

"'Kay, I'll take your word on that."

Betty Ann picked up a plastic cup of water sitting on the table next to Brid's feather and held it up with a questioning look. Jackie nodded and the nurse brought it close for her to sip from the straw.

"I'll bring a fresh jug in," she said, then fiddled with the tubes again before heading for the door.

Jackie spotted something on the floor.

"Excuse me," she said.

Betty Ann stopped.

"What's that?"

The nurse looked where Jackie was pointing and stooped to pick the object up. "Don't know. Looks like some kind of badge."

She handed it to Jackie, then continued out the door.

Jackie looked at the little piece of cloth – a Junior Forest Warden Fire Honour Badge. She turned her head and lay looking out the window at a flicker pecking eagerly at a tree trunk.

A few minutes later, her mother reappeared, carrying a food tray and a water jug. Jackie tucked the badge out of sight.

"Bumped into your nurse," Mary said, indicating the

tray. She set it in front of Jackie and removed the lid. The tray contained a couple of pieces of toast and a package of crackers. "She said just to try the crackers for now if you're feeling nauseous."

Mary settled into the chair closest to Jackie's bed and watched her. It seemed to Jackie that her mother wanted her to eat, so she took a cracker and nibbled it.

"Papa tells me I've given you the impression that I think you're weird."

Jackie swallowed.

"I guess I am a little weird." Her voice still made her sound like a drunken robot whose power source was weak.

Mary smiled. "Yes, but in a good way."

She held up a piece of toast for Jackie, but Jackie shook her head. Mary continued. "You're absolutely, one hundred per cent, exactly what you should be, Jackie. You're perfect."

Jackie looked at her mother. Wasn't she angry with her about the way she'd been treating Chris?

"Really?"

Mary nodded. "I guess sometimes I worry that I can't help you girls as much as I want to…. I feel like I haven't given you enough of what you need. I don't know what it's like to be you. And people in this world can be so awful."

As Jackie listened to her mother, it slowly dawned on

her. Mary didn't know what she had done. She didn't know that Chris had got his nose broken protecting her. He hadn't told anyone.

Jackie pushed the food tray away.

"Can't you eat any more than that?" Her mother looked anxious.

Jackie shook her head.

Jackie fell asleep with her mother stroking her hair. She didn't wake when the rest of the family returned, nor when they left again much later.

WHEN SHE NEXT WOKE, she knew several hours had passed from the way the light through the window had changed. She thought at first that she was alone, until the rocking chair moved and she saw that Papa was there watching her.

"Where is everyone?" she asked. Her voice was sounding more human. Her head also felt less like Spider Mapp was playing his drums inside it.

"Your mother will be back later. They took Sidney home to put her to bed. That child is somethin else."

Jackie searched for words. "She's a bit like an elf with super powers."

Papa smiled.

Silence grew around Jackie and her Papa, but it was a

warm, safe silence that made her feel like he would be with her forever.

Forever and ever.

"Papa," she said, "I know what that song is about now."

Some people might have had to ask, what song? but not Papa.

"Do you?"

"Yes. It's about making mistakes."

"Maybe. You could be right."

"Do you know why Chris was fighting?"

Papa shook his head no.

"I had some cigarettes from another kid and Chris didn't want me to get in trouble, so he said they were his."

Papa laughed. "That boy, he's somethin else too."

Jackie swallowed hard. A great, huge lump filled her throat. She swallowed and swallowed, but she couldn't keep the tears in.

Papa looked at her very gently. "Is Chris mad at you now?" he asked.

Jackie nodded.

"And you think he's gonna stay mad?"

Jackie nodded again and used her blanket to try to stop the tears from rushing down.

Papa gave her a box of tissues.

"All of us make mistakes," he said. "That's okay, long

as we try to put them right."

A voice came through the PA system behind Jackie's head, calling for Dr. Poulsen.

Papa crossed the room to close the blinds.

"Can I go see him?"

Papa looked doubtful.

"Please?"

"I'll ask somebody at the desk."

Jackie nodded.

EVEN WITH BETTY ANN LAMOUREUX and Papa's help, it took Jackie five minutes to get from her bed to the wheelchair.

What if he screams at me to get out? she wondered, as Papa wheeled her toward room J42 on the third floor. The hallway was lined with paintings of birds; one was an African Grey Parrot, Jackie noticed.

They heard voices from inside as they hesitated outside the room.

"Can I go in by myself, Papa?"

Papa said, "Sure," and indicated he'd be waiting in the lounge at the end of the hall.

A doctor was with Chris and Bob in Chris's room. Chris was sitting on the edge of the bed. They turned at her knock on the door.

"Come in," the doctor said, smiling. "We're all done here." She scribbled a few notes on a pad, patted Chris on the arm, and left them.

Chris was unrecognizable. His eyes were bruised, and the rest of his face, except for his mouth, was covered in a gauze bandage.

Bob smiled warmly at Jackie. So he didn't know, either.

"And how's our other patient?" he asked.

"I'm doing pretty good," she said.

A couple of moments of awkward silence passed.

Bob made an excuse about needing a coffee and left Jackie and Chris alone.

JACKIE HAD NEVER MADE MISTAKES as big as these before. Sidney had fixed the mistake that put Jackie's life in danger. The doctors had fixed the mistakes that led to broken noses and broken ankles. But what about the mistakes that led to Jackie and Chris not knowing what to say to each other now?

Chris sat looking down at his feet.

Jackie finally found the courage to break the silence.

"Does it hurt?"

"No.... How 'bout your foot?"

"No."

They were both lying.

"Chris," she said, "why didn't you tell anyone what I did?"

Long moments passed.

"Your mom and dad...." he started. "They're my dad's best friends. And if I told my dad, he'd probably be mad at you...and then maybe he'd be mad at them too...and I didn't want him to lose his best...." Chris's voice trailed off.

"Oh," she said.

She felt a twinge of disappointment. She'd thought he was going to say, "So you wouldn't get in trouble." And after he'd said that, she was going to say, "Thanks, but I plan on telling everyone the truth," and then he would say, "Okay," and she would go on to say, "Remember when we were little and we said we'd get married one day?" and he would say, "Yeah," and she would tell him, "We probably won't get married, but I want you to know I love you more than everything that has a name, and I'll never let you down again, and I'll be a better friend, and I'm sorry...and, and, and...."

But that conversation didn't happen. They just sat there. She would have to show him, not tell him. And she would, if he would let her. She had a whole lifetime ahead – time to be the kind of friend to Chris that he was to her. If he would let her.

But for now the silence grew and surrounded them both and was like a presence they could feel.

"I'm sorry," she whispered. "Really, really, really sorry."

He nodded.

"I guess I better go." Jackie slowly turned her wheelchair and aimed it for the door. She wondered if the way she was feeling now was the way her grandparents felt all the time – she felt old. And sick.

"Oh." Jackie halted her slow progress, and turned back to Chris. "You dropped this."

She opened her hand and held out the badge.

Chris's ears went pink.

She had the feeling he hadn't wanted her to know he'd been to see her. She wished there was something she could say to help him. She suddenly wished she hadn't mentioned the badge.

"Maybe, uhhm, somebody else dropped it...."she said awkwardly. "Maybe Sidney, or...." It sounded lame, she knew.

Still holding the badge, she turned again and manoeuvred her chair across the room.

"Maybe...Ziggy."

Jackie wheeled around to face him. Was he joking with her? Should she laugh?

His face, what she could see of it, showed no trace of emotion.

Maybe breaking his nose had caused him to lose his mind as well.

She spoke haltingly. "Ziggy...moved to...."

"Norway. I know. But she always liked my badge."

Jackie searched his eyes. They were completely circled by bruises – and completely unreadable.

He walked over to her and reclaimed his Fire Honour Badge.

"See ya later," she said, and he nodded.

She wheeled out the door.

JACKIE MADE IT halfway down the hallway toward the lounge where Papa was waiting before stopping to rest. She looked up and saw a small, curly-haired figure, dressed in pyjamas, staring at the picture of the parrot. With a stab of longing, Jackie thought of Sidney and Brid. Then her longing turned to surprise.

"Sidney! What are you doing here?"

Sidney turned and smiled at Jackie. "I couldn't sleep."

"How did you get here?"

Sidney gestured toward the end of the hallway.

"Mom and Dad are down there with Papa."

Jackie nodded.

"Wanna push me the rest of the way?" she asked.

"Okay, Sister."

Sidney gripped the handles of Jackie's wheelchair, and down the hall they rolled; together.

ACKNOWLEDGEMENTS

I WOULD LIKE TO THANK THE FOLLOWING PEOPLE for their time, advice, and encouragement:

Nic, Naomi, and Kimiko Martini; Rochelle and Jordan Lamoureux; Richina, Pauline, Darcy, and Dion Foggo; Brian and Anna Cooley and Mary Ann Wilson; Brianna, Kirsten, and Kayla Strong; Alesha Porisky and Joanne Towers; Heather Baxter; and, of course, Clem, Chandra, and Miranda.

I would also like to thank the other members of my family for their support, especially Shaylen for making me laugh.

I want to express my appreciation to the members of my book club for their intelligence and wisdom, to the GATE kids for being who they are, and to my editor, Barbara Sapergia, for her patience and insights.

I would like to thank Carolyn Plummer-Ayana for permission to quote from her wonderful song, "I've Only Known a Stranger," and the late Esther Phillips for her beautiful interpretation of the song.

Excerpts from the Junior Forest Wardens Green Tree Trailblazer Manual are reprinted by permission of the Alberta Junior Forest Warden Association.

ABOUT THE AUTHOR

CHERYL FOGGO's young adult novel *One Thing That's True* was a finalist for the 1997 Governor General's Award for Children's Literature, the Mr. Christie Book Award, the Blue Heron Book Award, and the R. Ross Annett Book Award. Her first book, the non-fiction title *Pourin' Down Rain,* was a finalist for the Alberta Culture Non-Fiction Prize. She has published short fiction and poetry, and has had theatre, television, and film scripts produced.

A Calgary freelancer since 1980, Cheryl Foggo received the 1998 Overall Achievement Award from the Black Achievement Awards Society of Alberta.

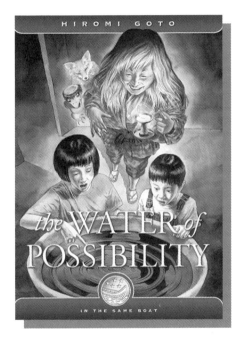

also in the series

IN THE SAME BOAT

CELEBRATING CANADIAN KIDS

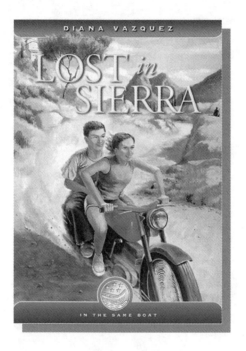

Lost *in* Sierra

by Diana Vazquez

A young Canadian girl unravels a family mystery
while visiting Spain.

also in the series

IN THE SAME BOAT

CELEBRATING CANADIAN KIDS

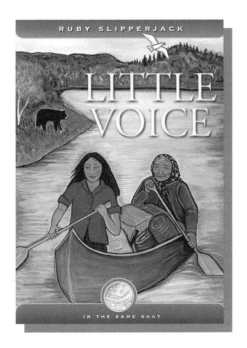

LITTLE VOICE
by Ruby Slipperjack

An Ojibwa girl comes of age during summers
spent in the bush with her grandmother.

also in the series

IN THE SAME BOAT

CELEBRATING CANADIAN KIDS

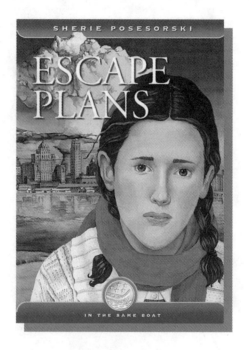

ESCAPE PLANS
by Sherie Posesorski

Thirteen-year-old Becky confronts her fears
at the height of the Cold War.

also in the series

IN THE SAME BOAT

CELEBRATING CANADIAN KIDS

JASON *and the* WONDER HORN

by Linda Hutsell-Manning

A magical horn transports three kids
back to medieval Germany.